ZACHARY

A DEMONS-IN-LAW NOVEL

LOUISA MASTERS

Zachary

Copyright © 2024 by Louisa Masters

Cover: Booksmith Design

Illustrated Paperback Cover Art: Christine Marie

Editor: Hot Tree Editing

A dragon with endless secrets meets a demon with nothing to hide…

I'm the easygoing one. The fun one. The rare member of my family who gets along with anyone. Except there's a chance I may have got off on the wrong foot with our new dragon liaison, Ronan. In my defense, he rubs everyone the wrong way. The only thing he's got going for him is his looks… if the miserable frown weren't there to mar them. But he seems to be trying harder to connect, and I guess I should do the same. Even if his arrival here was the beginning of all my problems.

When I cross the line and guilt compels me to apologize, I get my first glimpse of a different Ronan. Someone who enjoys baking, thinks glitter is amazing, and wants people to like him. Someone I could be friends with. And when that frown disappears? I want more than just friendship.

But there's something going on with him, something he's been carrying for a long time. He's been hurt before, and the secrets he's keeping are the kind that eat you inside. How can we take things to the next step if he can't be open with me?

It's only when he steps up to make all my dreams come true that I realize some secrets need to stay that way… and that loving Ronan means accepting him for who he really is.

CHAPTER ONE

Ronan

FEBRUARY

I STAND on the sidewalk and stare up at the building, ignoring the people jostling past me as they go about their lives. If I don't go in soon, I'll be late for my appointment with Brandt, but I can't seem to make my feet move.

It's not because I don't want to see Brandt—I do. Ever since that first meeting, when I looked at him and *knew* that he could make everything okay, I've always been eager to spend time in his company. I grew up with people doting on me, and I thought I knew what it was to belong, but I didn't—not until Brandt walked into the room—a room in this building—and a part of me I didn't even know was hurting cried out in relief.

Yet I still ignored it. For days, I ignored it. For days I clung to the lies I'd been raised on. To the memory of the people I thought cared about me. Until it was impossible to pretend any longer that my whole life hadn't been one giant fabrication, a charade meant to keep me docile and feed my rage against those I thought were my enemies—my own people.

My own brother.

The very people I was trying to hurt.

That broke me.

And every time I walk into this building, I'm flooded with guilt for the pain I caused. Guilt for the things done by those who raised me. Even though I've tried so hard, worked so hard to atone for those things over the past five years, this building brings all my shame crashing back.

I think Brandt knows, which is why we usually meet at Here Be Dragons, the estate outside the city that's the home base for all dragonkind, and why he apologized twice when he called to ask me to meet him here today. Which just adds to my guilt—Brandt should never have to apologize to me for anything. Not when I'll spend the rest of my life making up for the trouble I caused.

So I guess I shouldn't keep him waiting.

Sucking in a deep breath, I force my right foot to take the first step. That's always the hardest one.

Over these past years, anytime I've faced a situation I didn't want to walk into—and there have been many—I've always coached myself through the first step and found that the others came easier. Just like now. Across the sidewalk. Through the main door. The huge building lobby. There's even an elevator waiting, doors open, so I don't need to slow my momentum. I just step right in and make myself hit the button for the right floor. This is fine. I'm doing this.

Then I make the mistake of glancing up toward the other occupants of the elevator. Two are human and stare disinterestedly at their phones. The other two are not.

The incubus stares at me with wide eyes and presses himself back into the corner. I guess he's had a run-in with

Steffen in the past and isn't eager to repeat the experience. My identical twin can be… abrasive.

More guilt floods me as I remember why.

The elf, on the other hand, watches me with slightly narrowed eyes. I know him—well, I recognize him. He was there *that day*. One of the security team that responded when Wil sent out the intruder alert. He knows Steffen personally, works with him, and can tell the difference between us, now that I wear my hair a little longer.

I nod slightly and look away but can still feel his gaze burning into me. I don't blame him for not trusting me. Very few people know my story, and I doubt he's one of them. Only those with the highest security clearance and need-to-know status were told. Of course, with me and Steffen being identical, it was necessary to say *something*, but the official story is that I'm Steffen's long-lost twin brother —which is true—and that, while trying to meet him for the first time, had foolishly not announced myself. People thought I was him, and I just went with it.

Which is also true… mostly. At the time, I was going out of my way to make people think I was him. Regardless, I'm pretty sure this particular elf knows he didn't get the full story and doesn't trust me for a second. I don't blame him.

The elevator stops at my floor and the doors ding as they open. I step out and walk toward the reception desk. It's manned by a very cute elf who I know from my few previous visits is also very sassy. The elf from the elevator also gets off, but instead of swiping himself through the security gates into the main office or heading toward one of the meeting rooms, he moves into my line of vision, folds his arms across his chest, and hovers.

Message received, loud and clear.

The receptionist—Dáithí—looks up as I approach,

does a double-take, then smiles. "Ronan, right? Brandt said you were coming in. Take a seat and I'll let him know you're here."

"Thank you." The words are hoarse, and I clear my throat and smile back at him. He blinks, and I know from other people telling me in the past that he's surprised to see "Steffen's" face smiling.

I turn toward the row of visitor chairs, and Dáithí snaps, "What's your problem? Stop loitering in my space and go pretend you do some work around here."

Sitting, I peer surreptitiously at the security elf, who raises a brow at Dáithí but doesn't move or speak. He's basically between me and the reception desk right now, ready to strike if I… yell at Dáithí for the wait?

I mean, I know he's thinking along the lines of something more serious, and I really, really don't blame him—he has cause—but he just heard Dáithí say Brandt's expecting me.

"Ugh!" Dáithí throws up his hands in exasperation, then grabs—

I blink. Is he spraying the elf with a water bottle?

"Hey!" Yep, the security elf is stepping back, hands up in defense against the water. "Quit that!"

"Serves you right. Now get the mop and clean up that mess, then get to work," Dáithí orders. I study him with new eyes. Sassy is one thing, but this… This is a whole new level. Especially when the security elf meekly opens the door to a closet, brings out a mop, and begins swabbing the floor. He's still keeping one eye on me, but I'm impressed. I wonder if Dáithí can teach me that level of self-confidence.

I used to have it, until I discovered it was all built on the destruction of others.

The security gate opens, and Steffen steps out. I stand,

and we walk toward each other. It's like looking at myself... if I never smiled and considered nearly every living being to be a threat. At least he no longer looks at me that way—it's taken a long time, but sometimes I even get an almost-smile.

Then his gaze slides over to the elf with the mop. He nods to Dáithí and gestures to me. "Brandt's waiting."

My brother is a man of few words.

I smile again at Dáithí and follow Steffen through the gate, resisting the urge to look back at the security elf and twiddle my fingers in a wave. I used to do things like that when I was a very young child, and while my nurse thought it was adorable, *he* would chide me about behaving with dignity. I wanted nothing more than to make him proud, so I repressed the habit.

But since coming to Earth and spending time with other dragons, I've come to realize that kind of behavior is normal for us. We're... fun. And while I know my twin was broken in a way he can never fully heal from, if I'm going to devote my life to helping dragonkind, I need them to be able to relate to me. So... I'm learning to be fun again.

Trying to, anyway. It's not going all that well.

"How have you been?" I ask Steffen, keeping my voice low in deference to his preference for privacy. I spoke to him only a week ago, but I want him to know I care. Because I do, so much. It kills me sometimes that, as far as our relationship has come, it will never be what I used to dream about when I was small.

He gives a tiny nod. "Everything is well here." Hesitates, then adds, "I bought some new blades. I'll show you later."

My heart soars. Anyone else might think that's a weird thing to say, but I know Steffen now. He doesn't volunteer information. Doesn't participate in the art of conversation.

This is him *trying*. This is him showing me he wants to connect. "That would be great."

I leave it there—he's more comfortable with silence, and I don't want to push him. It's up to him how our relationship goes, not me.

We get to Brandt's office, and he knocks once before opening the door and walking in. I follow.

"Ronan," Brandt says warmly, getting up from behind his desk and coming around it. I glance at Steffen, who nods, then take three big, fast strides to meet Brandt and receive his hug. There is nothing in existence like the touch of the wing leader. All my stress, all my guilt… it falls away with the soothing touch of the life force.

It's not until I finally step back from the embrace that I realize there are others here. Wil doesn't surprise me—he's Steffen's second-in-command and probably closest friend. As much as Steffen has friends, anyway. But Fabian… usually I only see him at Here Be Dragons.

"Hi." I smile at them both and give a little wave. "It's good to see you." I mean it. These are some of the people Brandt knows and trusts the most, and when he first brought me home to Here Be Dragons, they were the ones who helped me, taught me what it meant to be a dragon. Fabian, especially—he's the species historian and record-keeper, and he spent dozens of hours patiently answering questions and telling me things about my own species that I never knew.

"You too," Wil says. "It's been a while—"

"Chat later!" Fabian's all but bouncing in his seat, a wide, excited grin lighting his face. "Tell him tell him tell him!"

"Take a breath," Brandt advises wryly, going back to his chair. "Ronan, have a seat. We've got some exciting news, and a project for you."

I sit, my curiosity piqued. A project? I'll do it, of course. Anything Brandt needs from me.

"There's been a discovery just outside the demon village of Hortplatz," Brandt begins, and I shake my head.

"I'm not familiar with it," I admit.

"There's no reason why you should be, especially this village. It's in Switzerland, and until very recently, the only people who lived there were demons."

That's a shock. The community of species is very well integrated—I didn't realize there were whole towns made up of a single species.

"Most of the reason for that is the location," Wil explains. "Most of the year, it's cut off by snow, and since demons can teleport in and out, they—"

"Pleeeeeeeease tell him the boring stuff later," Fabian begs. "Come *on.*"

Wil rolls his eyes, but he's smiling, and Brandt chuckles. Even Steffen's face softens… a little.

"All right, then," Brandt soothes. "Ronan, in one of the caves above the village, they discovered a twelve-ish-thousand-year-old vault door heavily protected by dragon preservation spells."

My jaw drops.

"That was my reaction too," Wil assures me.

"Steffen and I have been up there, and I have some photos I can show you," Brandt continues. "The door itself is also a lock—it's a giant mechanical puzzle. CSG has located an expert who will begin work on solving it any day now, and he believes he can have it open within a few months."

"This is incredible," I murmur, and it *is.* But I still don't know why I'm here. "Do, uh, do we know what's inside?" I'm struck by sudden dread that it's something of *his.* Even dead, he haunts me.

Brandt shakes his head, and I try not to sag in relief. "I recognized the magical residue of the dragon who created it all, and it could be anything. She had wide and varied interests. The point is, CSG, the DEA, and the village of Hortplatz have come to an agreement regarding the cave and its contents. Part of our responsibility is to provide a dragon to identify and catalogue the contents of the vault once it's open." He smiles at me.

My heart sinks. He can't mean…

"I think you'd be perfect for the job."

CHAPTER TWO

Zac

TWO WEEKS LATER

I PUSH my potatoes around my plate, only half-listening to the conversation around me. Most of my mind is on my plans for a ski resort—it's never been practical before, or the village council never believed it to be, but I know I can make it work. And if we're trying to attract people of other species to visit and live here, it's exactly what we need. At the very least, if the cave proves to be the kind of museum attraction everyone thinks it will be, the visitors will need places to stay and other things to do to keep them busy while they're here.

There is, however, a tiny part of my brain that's still smarting over the telling-off Garrett gave me this afternoon. Who cares if I didn't pat the dragon on the head and coo over his teleport sickness? That wasn't going to help him. What *did* help him was even breaths, time, and a few sips of water. But nooo, Garrett got all snotty about how I wasn't nice to Ronan while he was suffering. It's not like I called him a whiney baby or anything—which I wouldn't have. I'm not a monster. Some non-demons get teleport sick, and I *do* feel bad for them, but there's literally nothing that can be done. It passes after a few minutes, and that's what I said.

Which somehow convinced Garrett that I was about to fuck up demon-dragon relations for all time and destroy the cave project before we even get the door open. When I told him he was overreacting, he launched into a lecture about some king centuries ago who pissed a bunch of people off… I tuned out in the end. Garrett's great, and he's perfect for my cousin, but he sure does like to lecture.

I sneak a glance across the table at the dragon in question. Ronan. He's one of the twins, the less-scary-looking one—and coming from a demon, that's saying something. We're known for having stone faces. The truth is that tele-porting requires us to have a denser muscle mass that makes our facial expressions more subtle, which not all species can pick up on without trying. Some of us, like my cousin Gideon, *are* naturally grumpy, but most just seem like it to those not in the know. Steffen Draco, on the other hand, seems to have gone out of his way to cultivate a suspicious, intimidating glare. Which makes his twin, Ronan, the more attractive one—if not for the fact that he's spent the whole afternoon looking like he's on his way to his execution. When he wasn't battling nausea, that is.

Too bad. He's a very good-looking man, plus there's something fascinating about the different facial structure the dragons have. When I first saw him, I have to admit, I was… interested. I thought maybe him being a dragon wasn't going to be the most exciting part of his visit. But it only took a few minutes in his company for me to let that idea go. He's miserable.

It's… weird. Everyone else is excited about the cave. The dragon Fabian has been asking questions nonstop, chattering so much that Grandmother's eyes are starting to narrow. Even Ronan's scary brother seems interested. Ronan's acting like coming here is the worst punishment anyone could ever be given. I don't get it.

"You're sure you won't be staying longer than a few days?" Grandmother asks Fabian pointedly, and Garrett winces. It's pretty clear to those of us who know her that she's about five minutes of chatter away from a homicidal rampage, and from the way Steffen straightens in his seat, he's picked up on that.

"I can't," Fabian says regretfully. "Once the cave is open, I'll visit to check in on things, but I have other responsibilities. Plus, I couldn't leave my boyfriend for so long, and he can't get the time away from work. We haven't been apart for more than a few days in *years* and—"

"Your dedication is commendable," Grandmother cuts him off, then turns to Ronan. "You will be staying the entire time?"

Ronan drags his eyes from his plate and nods. "Yes, ma'am."

"Are you also an expert in dragon lore and history?"

"No, ma'am."

Grandmother waits for him to add more. He doesn't, returning his gaze to his food, and I brace.

"Why, then, does the wing leader feel you are the best choice to remain here?"

"Ronan's spent the last few years visiting dragon settlements and helping our people to feel more comfortable with leaving our homeland behind," Wil intercedes. If I had to guess, I'd say he's here to be the diplomat of the group. Too bad he's leaving tonight with Steffen. "Brandt believes that gives him a unique perspective in regard to your village."

Grandmother's brow rises slowly. "Because we need assistance to integrate with others?"

"I'd never presume to say so, ma'am, and that's not what our representative would be doing, anyway. You requested a dragon to help catalogue the contents of the vault, and that's what Ronan's here for."

"But he says he has no expertise in dragon history." She returns her gaze to Ronan. "Correct?"

"Yes."

"He's still a dragon," Steffen snaps, and suddenly the air is crackling with tension. Even Fabian is frowning.

Grandmother, for the first time in a long time, chooses not to push. "Of course. The wing leader knows what he's doing."

From two seats away, I hear Garrett's shaky exhale of relief as my mother changes the subject and conversation resumes. Ronan's face is even more miserable than before, if that's possible.

What the fuck is going on?

♏

ONE WEEK LATER

If I have to hear one more overenthusiastic rendition of an eighties hair band song from my cousins-in-law, I won't be responsible for my actions. Will karaoke night never end?

I hate my family.

No, scratch that. I hate my family, my village, and my whole fucking life. And I especially hate that mopey, miserable dragon. Ronan's been nothing but trouble since he got here, and it's only been six days. He's completely managed to fuck up my life just by existing.

First, there was the fact that Garrett volunteered me to

introduce him and Fabian around town. I honestly didn't mind that when I heard about it, and Fabian is a hoot. But Ronan manages to cast a shadow on everything and everyone. Can't he at least *pretend* he doesn't hate being here?

He pissed Grandmother off so much that she wouldn't even listen to my idea for the ski resort the next day. *"Stop wasting time on dreams, Zachary. The village needs you for more important things."*

My grandmother has never struck me, not even back when it was an acceptable form of discipline for children. At that moment, it felt as though she had. The village needs me for more important things? I do everything that's asked of me. There's no job description for ranger in Hortplatz, no salary… nothing. Officially, the role doesn't exist. And yet, I'm the one who fills it. I'm the one who makes sure the terrain around the village is safe. I'm the one who keeps track of the local wildlife. I'm the one who trains everyone in wilderness safety. I lead the search and rescue team *and* the local volunteer fire department.

Sure, I love that work, love being able to spend all my time outdoors in nature, but I'm sick of having it *expected* of me.

The village needs me for more important things? Then maybe the village should show some appreciation instead of taking me for granted. Because the only things keeping me here are family and duty, and I can always visit my family. But if nobody is ever going to let me have any input, I can't say my sense of duty won't run out.

I've been giving to this village my whole life. I learned an entire new ecosystem half a century ago so I could help this settlement get its best start. Nobody can tell me I haven't done my duty. All I want now is to help the village grow and prosper, and having that brushed aside as a foolish dream… well, fuck that.

And finally, Garrett and Cam came up with the asinine idea that they need to help me find "someone special."

So, yeah, I'm in a shitty mood. And yeah, I know my cousins and their men have guessed. Cam even cornered me about it earlier. I dodged him for a while, but then I thought, maybe I should tell him? Get it off my chest? He and I are friends—we would be even if he wasn't dating Micah. He wasn't born into our family, hasn't lived with Grandmother's pervasive opinions on duty for his whole life. Maybe his is the perspective I need. Maybe he could give me some ideas for how to approach it again or even just validate whether I'm doing the right thing.

Except that was when Arne at the pub interrupted to complain about Ronan. Fucking Ronan. Who managed to upset half the town so much within just a few days that they actually want him out. That's going to be *great* for future demon-dragon relations.

Garrett and Asher went to talk to him and said Ronan was going to fix things, but by then, Cam was all distracted and stressed—the cave project is his baby—and he'd forgotten all about me and my problems. Not that I'd admitted to him that I *had* problems, but still.

"It might be time we call it a night," Asher suggests hopefully as the last note of "I Drove All Night"—the Celine Dion version, Garrett informed us as though we cared—finally dies away. "It's late, and we want to be on our game tomorrow when Ronan starts apologizing to people."

Garrett stands immediately. "Yes. And we're all going to be supportive, right? This can't be easy for him. We practically had to ask him straight-out if he was speciesist." He stares pointedly at me.

"I've been nothing but supportive," I say flatly. My family looks doubting. "What? I introduced him to everyone and answered his questions. I'm not the one who's such an ass to everyone that people thought he was speciesist."

"Maybe don't help tomorrow," Asher advises. "You've had a busy week. You deserve a day to yourself."

That would mean more if I didn't know he doesn't trust me not to make the situation worse. A situation I had nothing to do with causing in the first place. I change the subject. "So who's the tournament winner?"

As Cam and Garrett immediately begin bickering over that, I head toward the stairs and the sanctuary of my suite. Micah stops me. Asher's attempting to referee the dispute, and we have a rare moment of privacy.

"I haven't had a chance to talk to you this week," my cousin says, "about the ski resort project you were working on last Sunday. Have you had a chance to find someone to do a land survey?"

My heart stutters. This is my chance. Micah's like my brother. He loves me, and he believes in me. Better, he's an engineer, and if he thinks the idea's feasible, the council will listen. I open my mouth to tell him I need his support—

"Micah, tell them I'm the best diva!"

He's instantly diverted by Cam's voice, and my hope fades. Micah's like my brother. He'd back me on this, but he's got other priorities right now, and it would be selfish of me to demand his time. Already he's juggling his regular job with Grandmother's demands. "I shelved the project," I say. "Go help Cam."

He frowns, and it looks like he's going to ask a question, but the volume of the "discussion" rises, and my cousin goes to rescue his boyfriend.

And I go to bed.

CHAPTER THREE

Ronan

After Garrett and Asher leave, I sit for a long time staring at nothing. It's only when my limbs begin to cramp that I blink and realize how much time has passed. It's become dark.

Automatically, I stand to go turn the lights on—and freeze. Light switches are an old habit, from when my magic was mostly bound, from when I'd been trained not to rely on it. Sitting down again, I use magic to flip the light switch. I could avoid the light switch altogether and use my magic to light the room, but that would be unnecessary. What's the point of living in this new world if I'm not willing to be part of it?

Which brings me right back to the reason for Garrett's impromptu visit: my failure. I haven't even been here for a full week, and already I've failed at this task Brandt set me. The only thing he's asked of me, other than my oath not to harm his people and allies, back when I was still considered an enemy prisoner. Since then, he's homed me, fed, clothed, comforted. Taught. Helped me to continue when I was convinced I couldn't. I vowed that I would spend my life atoning for the destruction I was, even unknowingly, part of, but Brandt never asked it of me. He asked me what I wanted and how he could help me get it, but this, representing him here in Hortplatz—this is the only thing he's ever asked me to do.

And the people here hate me so much, they want me to leave.

Garrett didn't say that, of course. He was very gentle, very diplomatic. Suggested that perhaps I was finding it a challenge to acclimate to the colder weather. Said that people had noticed I was a little down-spirited… that maybe I wasn't used to associating only with demons? And if that was the case, nobody would be offended if I preferred to ask for a replacement.

It was no surprise that people have noticed my mood—though I wince to think how rude I've been, inflicting it on them—but the hint that I might be speciesist, that shocked me to my core. I *was* raised that way. Raised to believe in a class system among elves that simply does not exist in reality, and then, when the need to migrate to Earth became critical, taught that Earth species were subordinate. I've worked hard, so hard to overcome those teachings, and I genuinely don't believe them anymore. How can I, when I've seen and worked firsthand with other species who are far more intelligent and talented and capable than I am? More learned, certainly.

Not that it would be hard to be more learned than I am. I barely know the basic facts of my own people, much less the complex languages and histories of others and concepts of engineering and mathematics.

I remember those moments in Brandt's office after he said he wanted me to identify and catalogue the contents of the cave.

"Me? That's impossible."

For once, the flash of his smile does nothing to soothe me. "There are few things that are truly impossible. This isn't one of them."

"But I'm the worst *choice! What about Fabian? This is his area of expertise."*

The room is quiet. Nobody's ever heard me argue with Brandt before. It's never happened before.

Brandt doesn't seem to care—or notice. He shrugs. "Fabian will consult, of course, but this will be a long process, and he can't be away from his regular duties to the living archive for such an extended period. He also tells me he'd miss Rhys too much."

"He gets lonely without me," Fabian explains. "There won't be anyone to listen to him explain all his TV shows. Plus, I need regular sex or my brain gets itchy."

"As long as it's not anything else that's itchy," Wil murmurs, and Fabian rolls his eyes.

"That's a human thing, Wil. Dragons can't catch STIs."

I make a mental note to look up what an STI is—humans are the species I have the fewest interactions with—but keep my attention on Brandt. He can't really mean to have me do this. "Someone else, then. Anyone else."

"I think you're the best choice."

My head shakes wildly, and I struggle to keep from trembling. "How can I be? How could I catalogue the contents of a dragon vault when I'm so ignorant of dragon history and culture?"

"You're not ignorant," Steffen begins angrily, and some of my frustration and fear lessens. My brother is defending me—even if it is against myself.

"Steffen's right," Brandt interrupts. "You are not ignorant, Ronan. Not every dragon knows every thing about dragonkind, and the fact that you know less is because your birthright was stolen from you. That's exactly why I think this will be good for you. The control of discovery will be in your hands—you'll be the first person in thousands of years to lay eyes and hands on whatever is found. You'll photograph, record details, and then, with the assistance of Fabian

and the archive, you'll identify. But we don't expect everything inside to be of dragon origin. The dragon who designed the cave was a great lover of Earth. She may have used it to collect objects from the native species, in which case, you'll be coordinating with the hellhound in charge of the project to bring in species historians and experts." He meets my gaze steadily. "This is a learning opportunity for you, Ronan. The chance to fill all the gaps you believe you have."

I stare back at him, panic a sick weight in my stomach. For all the logic in his explanation, I still know this is a mistake. Me, acting as representative for all dragons? The first dragon this village will come to know? How can I represent a species I sometimes don't truly feel I've earned the right to be part of?

And what if someone asks me a question about dragons or dragon history that I can't answer?

"Please, Ronan."

I swallow hard, unwilling to refuse Brandt. "Of course."

Bitterly, I wonder if Brandt would still have been so sure of sending me here if he'd known how badly I'd ruin things before the cave has even been opened.

The cave isn't open yet.

Like a blow, the reminder knocks the self-pity from me. That's right. Cam, the sweet incubus who was so excited to meet dragons, is still working on the mechanical puzzle that acts as a lock… and door. It was impressive to see, even if at the time I was both sick from teleporting and intimidated by the dragon who designed it. I could never do anything as amazing as that.

But it's still closed. Which means I have time to fix things. I *need* to fix them. Even aside from my assurance to Garrett that I've been distracted by problems from home and definitely *do* want to be here. That I'm looking forward to learning all I can about demons and their culture and will make certain I make amends with everyone who might think otherwise. I can't let this failure reflect poorly on my species—on Brandt. On my brother, who's had so many of his own hurdles to overcome and still manages to function within the community.

So… the first thing I need to do is make sure everybody knows I'm not speciesist. Then I can work on building up goodwill. By the time Cam has the door open, people will be *happy* to have me here.

I just don't know how to do that.

How do I even approach these people again? They hate me. And worse, dealing with demons is *hard*. Garrett warned me that their faces can be hard to read because of their heavier muscle mass, and I've been terrified ever since that I'm misinterpreting what they're saying.

I need advice. Fumbling my phone out of my pocket, I stare at it. Who would I even call about this? Usually when I need advice, I ask Brandt, my wingleader—my savior. But I'm not willing to let him know how badly I've mangled this already. I'm not exactly awash with friends… and anyway, I was told that at this stage in the process, the project shouldn't be discussed too widely.

I call my brother.

"If you're being hunted, don't say anything. This line isn't secure."

It took me a while, but I'm now used to having him answer the phone this way. Apparently his paranoia is much better than it used to be, but it will never completely go away.

"I'm not being hunted." Not yet, anyway. Thankfully, I didn't offend anyone quite that much. "But I've made some mistakes and I need advice." I explain the situation. "So what do I do next?"

"Give me some names," he says promptly. "Let me investigate these people and see if there's anything shady going on. They might be causing this fuss to drive you out because they know you can discover their secret plot."

I'm about to ask what secret plot but hear Wil in the background. "Who are you talking to?"

"Ronan," Steffen says. "The villagers are causing him trouble."

"No, that's not exactly right," I start, but Wil's already talking.

"Let me talk to him. Don't start investigating anyone yet. Let's get some more details first."

As usual, I'm impressed by the calm way Wil deals with Steffen's paranoia. He never talks down to him or makes it sound like he's being ridiculous. His respect for my brother —and protectiveness of him—are what I like best about him.

A second later, Steffen says, "You're on speaker, Ronan. Wil's here. Tell him what you told me."

I repeat my story, feeling shame well up. I know I can trust Wil, but it's still not fun telling him how poorly I'm doing at the first job Brandt's ever given me.

"It sounds like a simple misunderstanding," he says thoughtfully. "I know you've been… unhappy about having to be there, and they probably misread that."

I swallow hard. Great. I guess I'm even worse at hiding my feelings than I thought. "Yes. But… how do I fix it?"

"An apology, I guess? I might not be the best person to ask—I've been a soldier for six thousand years, and we used to just fight it out and buy each other a drink after."

"One of them owns the pub," I mumble glumly.

"Then that might actually work," he surprises me by saying. "Go see them all, tell them you had to move in a rush and leave some stuff unfinished at home, or something that they can relate to and sympathize with. You've been distracted and you realize you haven't made a great first impression, but you're excited to be there. Then tell them you want to make it up to them by paying for their first drink next time they're at the pub. Anyone who accepts the offer has forgiven you. The publican definitely will—just make sure you organize the tab with him before any of them turn up to cash in."

"Apologize, get sympathy, offer drink," I repeat. "You're sure that will work?"

"Positive. Anyone who's still mad after that has other issues, and we can work on them individually. Just make sure you say *first* drink. You don't want to be paying for the whole town's drunken night out."

He has a point there. Though maybe getting the whole town drunk will help them like me more.

CHAPTER FOUR

Zac

TWO WEEKS LATER

I THOUGHT the only thing worse than having my
grandmother slap down my ideas was when she slapped
me down—metaphorically—in public a week later,
demanding I fulfill my duty to the village and community
because I have nothing better to do. I was wrong, though.
Worse than that is having to spend my days with Ronan
Draco.

Damn his handsome, sexy, uptight self.

Finally I understand the human concept of Karma. I
was a prankster as a young demon, and now I'm being
punished.

The rest of the village may have been mollified by his
apologies and bribe—I have to admit, that was clever. And
to give him credit, he *is* trying harder with them. But now
that we're spending most of our time in the cave and vault,
just him, me, and sometimes Garrett, his true nature is
really shining through.

And that true nature is repressed, snobbish, and irritating.

That's okay. I don't need to be his best friend.

But it does mean that if Garrett's not with us, our days are mostly spent in silence. At first, that was fine. Monday, we came back to town to look something up, only to find out Cam had been kidnapped. Then, Tuesday and Wednesday, while we were still waiting for the satellite hookup to be organized, the day was a mess of Ronan needing to get back to cell access and being teleport sick every single time. It usually gets better the more often someone is teleported, but either dragons are an exception to that, or he's faking it for sympathy.

He won't get any from me.

So yeah, by the time Thursday rolled around and we finally had internet access in the cave and didn't have to travel back and forth so much, I was glad for the peace and quiet. I set myself up in one of the folding chairs and got back to reading some of the journal articles I've fallen behind on with all the chaos lately. Winter is usually the time I write my research findings and read everyone else's. For all that Grandmother and the village council seem to think I'm just a glorified woodsman, I'm actually a pretty respected geologist and botanist. My research in these mountains has been published in several peer-reviewed journals.

Now, though, it's midafternoon on Saturday, and I don't think Ronan's spoken a single word all day. Last night he said "Thank you" when I took him home, but thinking back on it, that might have been the only thing he said to me yesterday. I might like being alone in the outdoors, where I have nature and animals to keep me company, but I *am* still a people person. I grew up in a big, noisy family, and I'm used to having people drop in to see me and chat and ask favors most days. This silence is starting to get on my nerves.

Plus, it's Saturday. I'm drawing the fucking line.

Slapping the magazine I just finished reading down on the trestle table beside me, I stand and call, "Ronan?" as I walk toward the vault. My setup isn't that far outside, but we've made sure to leave clear the area needed for the door to close—we close it every night, remove the handle, and take it with us. It's incredibly unlikely that anyone would come here, especially in winter—but we're taking no chances with the contents of the vault.

Garrett, in his role as project coordinator, drew up a security plan for when we're working and had Gideon review it. The main part of the plan is that only authorized people have access to the cave and vault. The door is to be closed when the cave is unattended, with the handle removed to "lock" it. There's another whole procedure about how and where the handle can be stored overnight. The only people permitted to have possession of the handle are Ronan, Garrett, Cam, or, in the event of them being incapacitated, me. However, I'm not permitted to enter the vault itself unless Ronan needs my assistance or I need to remove an unauthorized person who somehow got in.

This is serious business.

Some people might not think we discovered treasure, but the historical artefacts Ronan's found and documented in just a few days are priceless beyond words. Some of them are from a settlement in Patagonia that was considered a center of knowledge and learning for our community—right up until it was destroyed during the species wars. Nobody's going to risk damage or theft to this treasure.

I stop at the threshold to the vault. "Ronan?" I call

again. I know he heard me the first time. The cave is big, but I wasn't that far away, and it's quiet in here.

A second later, he appears from the shadows at the back of the vault. Can dragons see in the dark? What was he doing back there?

"Yes?" He doesn't quite meet my gaze and stops walking when he's still ten feet away.

"Time for us to go." I don't waste any effort on pleasantries, and it's satisfying to see his blink of surprise. He looks at the iPad in his hands.

"But it's only three o'clock."

"On a Saturday. There's only so much work I'm willing to do on a weekend." That's not strictly true, but he doesn't need to know that. "We'll come back Monday morning."

"Monday?" His protest is loud. "What about tomorrow?"

"Weekend," I remind him. "Days off. Use the time to remind people how thrilled you are to be here."

Ronan's eyes narrow as my sarcasm hits home. For a second, I think he's going to say something, argue, but then he takes a deep breath. "Fine. Just let me put away the artefact I was examining." He turns to go back the way he came.

"In the dark?" My skepticism is clear. "If you're sitting back there sulking about how much you hate it here, I don't care, but don't keep me waiting too long."

For the first time since I met him, the unhappy expression completely falls away, replaced by something else: rage. He gestures, and suddenly there's a glowing light in front of him. It's the weirdest thing I've ever seen—the light seems to be completely contained within a radius of about ten inches, ending sharply, not disrupting the shadows on the other side at all. It's like the perfect directional light tool.

"The preservation spells are excellent, but we don't know the effect too much light might have on some of these artefacts," Ronan says. "Until everything has been identified, I thought it best to take precautions."

He walks away while I'm still trying to find words.

ᘻ

THE ANNOYING KNOWLEDGE that I need to apologize to Ronan is still gnawing at me hours later as I finish eating dinner. When I got home, the house was already brimming with the amazing smell of Älplermagronen. Cam fell in love with the dish after trying it at the pub, and today he attempted to make it himself—and did a pretty good job.

I scrape up the last of the potato, eat it, and say, "Happy to be your guinea pig anytime, Cam."

He grins at me, but it's not quite right. He's been acting a little odd ever since I got home. Maybe he's still feeling the effects of having been kidnapped by his stalker earlier this week.

"I'm going to hold you to that," he assures me, swiping his mop of curls out of his eyes. "Now, I believe there's a rule about the cook not having to do the washing up."

"That's fair." It's definitely a rule I enforce when I do the cooking—which is a lot. I like to cook, though sometimes it doesn't always work out the way I plan. "Go put your feet up, and we'll handle this."

"I need Garrett," he says hurriedly, gaze darting to Micah and then back to me. "For, um… stuff."

Okay… that's not weird at all.

"We can manage without Garrett," Micah declares brightly, which has me turning an incredulous look on him. Since when is Micah cheerful about washing dishes?

"Yep!" Asher adds. "We're big, strong demons. The three of us can handle anything."

Cam and Garrett practically flee the kitchen while I accept that this is a setup and I'm now officially trapped.

"Well?" I ask my cousins, who are both watching me patiently. "I swear, if this is because those two"—I tilt my head toward the door, where I'm pretty sure they're both listening—"have found someone they want to set me up with, I'm going to—"

"What's going on with you?" Asher's quiet voice cuts through my threat.

"What? Nothing." Fuck. I should have known they wouldn't let this go. It's been a week since they cornered me in the cave, and I thought I was in the clear. Stupid.

"Zac." Micah folds his arms. "C'mon."

"Don't, okay? I'm fine. I know I've been grouchy, and I'm sorry. This winter's getting to me, I guess."

"You've said that before, but we know it's bullshit. Usually when winter starts to make you feel hemmed in, you go camping in the snow."

He's right, and I think longingly about how great that would be—digging myself into a snowbank and creating a cozy little burrow. There's something spectacular about camping in conditions like this. At this altitude, so far from any chance of help, only a demon with teleport ability who's also highly experienced in the wilderness could ever expect to be able to do it safely, and it feeds the part of me that loves this planet so much.

"Yeah, well, it's not like there's been any opportunity for that this year." The second the bitter words leave my mouth, I regret them. My cousins exchange a glance. It's true that between the hubbub of Asher's wedding, the plans Garrett was making even before we discovered the cave, and then everything that's happened since, life hasn't exactly been able to run in its usual smooth track. Not for us, anyway, not with Grandmother insisting her family be involved in every aspect of the village. But it's not just me who's been affected, and nobody else is whining about it.

"Grandmother's been unfair to you," Asher says, shocking me. "She's always expected us to drop everything and leap to her bidding, but you most of all."

I shake my head. "No. She's hard on all of us."

Asher looks like he wants to argue, but Micah interrupts. "She was still wrong to saddle you with Ronan, especially after Brandt offered last week to have an elf assigned to transport him."

That's true, but… "One of us would still need to be there. The elves and dragons aren't familiar with the area or the altitude." The last thing we need is for our visiting representatives to get sick or injured up there. Although, I wonder if dragons can even get altitude sickness.

"And it could have been one of us," Asher counters. "Garrett and Cam are going to be spending a lot of time up there. But we don't want to argue about this. We just want you to know that whatever's wrong, you can tell us."

"Cam's worried about you." Micah raises a brow at me, knowing that will pile on the guilt. Cam's been through enough this week without having me to worry about.

I sigh. "I'm not happy with the way Grandmother just assumes my time belongs to her or the village or whoever she thinks needs it," I admit. "It bugs me. And I hate that if I push back, she throws duty in my face. I've done my duty for years. I'm *doing* my duty. I'm not trying to avoid it. But sometimes I just want…" I trail off. They're nodding. They get it. If anyone understands, it's them—they're in the same boat.

Maybe I should tell them what Grandmother said about the ski resort plans. With their support…

No. The part of me still stinging from the rejection pushes down the urge. The cave takes priority for now, along with the need to attract more people from other species to live in Hortplatz. There's a lot to do and a lot of expense involved in getting things ready for what Garrett has planned. Once the thaw sets in and the snow starts to clear, I'm going to be rushed off my feet with the additional tasks on top of my usual job. The ski resort is a pipe dream and needs to stay on the shelf for now.

"If you want to take a few days, go camping, we can cover for you," Asher offers. "Grandmother doesn't have to know."

I snort, and Micah laughs outright. As if anything happens around here that she doesn't know about.

Asher shrugs sheepishly. "I mean, she'd *know*, but we wouldn't have to tell her," he defends.

"Thanks, but I'm okay. I think I've convinced Ronan to take weekends off from now on." Or I might be able to, once I've apologized for my comments this afternoon.

They exchange glances again. Oh boy.

"What?" I ask.

"Why do you hate him so much?" Micah spreads his hands. "Garrett says you turn into Mr. Hyde around him."

It takes me a second to understand the reference. "Evil murdering criminal as opposed to mild-mannered scientist? How flattering."

"You know what he means. From that first day when he got teleport sick, it's been clear you don't like him. And fine, whatever—you don't have to. But do you have to make it so obvious?"

"It's not that I don't like him."

They both look at me like I'm an idiot.

"It's not. We don't get along, but that's not all on me. Yeah, him being here is inconvenient for me—and that's not his fault, I know. But he's so… I mean, this is the opportunity of a fucking lifetime, and he acts like he's being punished. If he's allowed to do that, why—" I stop, realizing how whiney and childish I sound.

"Why can't you? Fuck, Zac." For the first time since this conversation started, Asher's sympathy slips. "Ronan started out badly, we all know it. But he's trying now. We don't know his story—maybe this *is* a punishment for him. Maybe he's got a million things going on in his life that he wants to get back to, just like you do. It's not his fault he gets teleport sick. It's not his fault you're stuck babysitting him. You don't have to be his friend, but please, if only so Garrett and Cam stop worrying about it, please be civil to him. We all have so much riding on this project."

Hello, guilt.

"I'll be civil," I promise quietly. They have a point. I've been taking my shitty mood out on a lot of people lately, but they're all family and friends who'll call me an asshole to my face. Making snide comments to Ronan, who's a guest here and completely dependent on us—me—that's not fair.

"Okay," Micah says. "Let's leave it here. Even though we know there's still something else bugging you."

I open my mouth to deny it, then close it again. Why bother? They won't believe me, and they'll be right. "I'm not ready to talk about it."

Asher stands and begins stacking plates. "We're here when you are."

CHAPTER FIVE

Ronan

I WAKE up on Sunday morning with a terrifyingly empty day looming ahead of me.

Last night, even though Zac returned me to town earlier than usual, I managed to fill the time with my usual routine: meticulously checking my notes from the day, adding and changing things as needed, uploading them to the project server, and then sending a report to Fabian and Brandt. They've both told me they don't need daily reports, but it makes me feel better to let them know what I'm doing every step along the way, so they can stop me before I make any monumental mistakes.

Though truthfully, I'm not sure either of them even read the reports. Especially Fabian. He and the other expert historians who have access to the server are definitely looking at the photos and notes of each item, though, and adding their own notes as things are either identified or new possibilities are introduced. I've been checking those carefully, trying to learn as much as possible about the artefacts from each culture so my future notes can be more comprehensive and useful.

After I'd done that, I went down to the pub for dinner. I make a point of going at least twice a week now, even though I'd rather eat in the privacy of the house I've been assigned instead of sitting alone at the bar. But I don't want people to think I'm speciesist, so I order a counter meal, talk to Arne when he has time, and make sure to say hello to anyone who looks my way.

A few of them were wary at first, after everything they'd heard about me, but the people I apologized to personally always come over for a chat, and that's convinced the rest that I'm not that bad. It's even gotten easier to read their expressions, most of the time, though I think I'm going to need a lot more practice to be good at it. Wil was right to suggest buying everyone a drink. I'll have to remember that for the future.

Last night, the pub was especially busy, and I managed to loiter for several hours before it seemed as though everyone who was going to talk to me already had. I thought about trying to initiate conversation with someone or maybe seeing if I could join the group playing darts—I've only played once, and it was fun—but what if nobody wanted me around?

It was easier to go home and go to bed.

But now I'm awake at my usual early time, and the empty hours stretch terrifyingly ahead. Zac made it very clear yesterday that we wouldn't be going to the cave today. He made other things perfectly clear, too. Not that it was terribly surprising that he dislikes me—aside from his initial warm greeting, he hasn't exactly been welcoming— but I didn't realize his opinion of me was so low that he thought I'd be shirking work on such an important project.

Does he think I don't know how important history is? It's *everything*. The truth about the past is the most important thing there is.

I push aside my hurt feelings. Does it matter what one demon thinks?

Yes.

I ignore that voice. The rest of the town no longer hates me… mostly. Maybe later I can go for a walk and smile at some more people. Never mind that for the past weeks, I've really wanted to see Zac smile at me again the way he did when we met. For that one moment, it felt like sunshine was cutting through the gloom in my head.

Whatever. That's fanciful nonsense and a waste of my time. It's obvious that Zac wants weekends off, and so I'm going to need to find some way to fill those days.

Like studying.

I sit up in bed. The room is still dark in the early dawn, but I don't bother turning on a light. I don't need to see. I need to *think*. There's so much I don't know about, even my own species' history, even though I've been trying to learn, desperate to feel more like a real dragon. It's had to take a backseat to my other work the past few years, my focus mainly on repaying the debt I owe the universe. But with two whole days off every week, maybe I can make headway on that—or on learning about some of the Earth cultures. My understanding of them is very rudimentary, just what's needed to help other dragons feel like they would be able to make a connection with their new neighbors.

It's ironic that I struggle so hard to make that same connection myself.

But maybe if I knew more… And which species would be better to start with than demons? I'll be here in Hortplatz for a few months more, at least. Possibly longer if my fears are correct and Brandt plans to make me a permanent liaison to the museum.

Please don't let him do that.

I push the thought aside. I can worry about it later. For now… leaning across, I grab my phone from the nightstand and squint at the sudden brightness of the screen. If I'm calculating the time difference correctly, it's just after midnight Saturday night at Here Be Dragons. Fabian might still be up, and he's the best person to ask for resources to learn about demons.

I don't want to wake him if he's sleeping, though, so I send a text message instead.

> I'm interested in learning about demons. Could you recommend some books or websites?

There. Even if he doesn't see it for hours, at least I've made a start. In the meantime, I can go through all the notes on the artefacts that have been catalogued so far, see if there's anything new. Maybe do some side research on what's been identified. That would help to fill the day.

My phone dings.

> I'm confused. Aren't you in a town populated only by demons right now?

> Yes. That's why I want to learn more about them.

I regret sending that immediately. I know what he's going to say next.

> Why do you need books when you can ask them?

Shit. I stare at the screen for a long moment.

> Good point. Never mind.

Then I change my mind.

> Actually… there were some small problems before. With me. And the villagers. It's mostly fixed, but

My clumsy thumb hits Send before I can finish the sentence. It's probably just as well, since I don't know what I'd even say.

Turns out, I didn't need to tell him more.

> Oh that's right. Wil mentioned some people were upset.

And my humiliation is complete. Wil told everyone?

I shake my head, mostly to clear my thoughts. No. Wil wouldn't do that. He doesn't gossip, not like some of the others. He probably told Fabian because he's involved in the project… which means he definitely told Brandt.

My breath hitches. So Brandt knows I nearly fucked things up beyond repair. My eyes sting, and I blink hard. This is fine. Wil would also have told him that I fixed it. He knows I'm trying not to let him down.

I hope.

My phone dings again.

> You don't need books, you need to get out and connect with people. Trust me.

I want to throw the phone in frustration. Doesn't he get it? I'm not him. Fabian can talk to anyone. I've heard the story of the time he planned a fancy dinner for Rhys, his boyfriend, and a group of strangers at the store rallied together to help him. People like him. They can't help themselves.

I'm the opposite.

Swallowing hard, I make myself reply.

> It's not that easy.

I can't bring myself to explain. Dragons are by nature gregarious. Even the quieter ones, like Wil, are fun to be around. Steffen and I are the only exceptions I've ever heard of—him because he was tortured for hundreds of years until his brain evolved to protect him.

And me? I'm not a real dragon. Not in the ways that matter. I don't even have a hoard.

The loud trill of my phone ringing makes me jump. Fabian's name is on the screen, and for a second, I consider not answering. Unfortunately, he's not the kind to give up.

"Hello?"

"Don't worry, I got you," he assures me confidently, not bothering with a greeting. "This is just like sex."

I blink in the dawn gloom of the room and wonder if I'm actually still asleep and dreaming. "It… is?" How? Nothing I've ever heard about sex points to any connection.

"Sure. There's people like me, who have sex all the time. Before I met Rhys, I'd have sex with anyone I was attracted to. It was fun and I liked it and was good at it. But people like Rhys prefer to have sex with people they know and have romantic interest in. Neither of us was wrong; we just viewed sex differently."

I nod, even though I know he can't see me. "Okay. I get that. But how is—"

"I'm a person who likes talking to strangers," he continues in his blithe Fabian way. "Even when they don't like me, I still talk to them because I want to know why. *Why* is everything."

"Is there anyone who doesn't like you?" I ask curiously.

He hesitates. "Um. Yes? Maybe. Does it count if they didn't like me before but they do now?"

I don't know if I want to sigh or laugh. "Sure. That counts."

"Great! So, anyway… what were we talking about?"

"You like talking to strangers," I prompt. "And it's just like sex."

"Eww, no, Ronan. Talking to strangers isn't like having sex. I mean, sure, they're both fun, but it's in very different ways. Maybe you need to think about the kind of sex you're having. If your partners aren't meeting your needs—"

Panic drives me to interrupt. "I misspoke! You were comparing my current situation to the fact that people have different views toward sex."

He stops. "I was? Oh! Yeah. So I'm a person who likes talking to strangers, but you're not. So it's harder for you to connect with people you don't know."

The echo of my earlier thoughts is both comforting and hurtful. He'd never say it aloud—he's not cruel—but even Fabian thinks I'm not a real dragon.

"Yes," I manage.

"I can help," he assures me. "First step is to make a better connection with the people you already know. Who do you spend the most time with?"

Um. I know what he's getting at, but—

"Ronan? You still there?"

"Yeah. Uh, I guess in total number of hours, that would be Zac, the demon who comes to the cave with me. But—"

"Perfect! He's nice, and you're already spending all that time together with nobody else to make you feel self-conscious or distract you. There's plenty of opportunity to build a friendship, or at least a friendly acquaintanceship. And he's one of Gideon Bailey's cousins, isn't he? That family has a lot of influence there."

I let him finish, wondering just how I'm going to explain this. "They do, but—"

"So what you need to do is think about what you already know about Zac, like his interests or hobbies. Or you could ask him what he did last night—that's always a good opener. What time are you meeting him today?"

"I'm not—he said we're taking weekends off. Uh… Zac might not be the best person for this. He doesn't like me." My cheeks burn with embarrassment as I force myself to make the confession.

"He doesn't?" Fabian sounds confused. "Why not?"

What's worse, knowing someone dislikes you for a reason, or just having them dislike you because you're *you*? Because I remember how Zac was when Fabian was still here—a little distracted, not quite as friendly as his cousins, but it was still clear that he liked him. It's just me he has a problem with.

"I don't know," I mumble, wishing I'd never sent that text. How hard could it have been to find some resources on my own? Now Fabian will tell Brandt how unlikeable and un-dragon I really am.

"Okay. Don't worry, I've still got you covered," he rallies. "You're not going to the cave today, right? So you've got some time to prepare. Think about the people in town who've been nicest to you, and make a list of what you know about them. If you feel up to it, maybe go and talk to one of them. But it's okay if you're not ready!"

I waver, trying to decide if I should just tell him to forget the whole thing. "I was going to go over the research notes today—"

"Nope! No work. You need some time to recharge. Zac was right to say weekends off."

I hear someone laugh in the background and realize

with a little shock that his boyfriend is there. Of course he must be, this late. They live together.

"I'm so sorry, I've interrupted your evening—"

"You haven't. We were just watching one of Rhys's shows that he's seen a million times before. And I'm *not* a workaholic, Rhys. I take plenty of time off. Just sometimes I get very involved in things and forget other stuff."

Remembering the number of times Fabian had to be fetched for meals while I was living at Here Be Dragons, and when he strolled nonchalantly out into the snow without shoes because he was distracted by his thoughts, my mood lifts. We all have our little eccentricities. Mine is just… less dragonish than everyone else's.

"No work today," Fabian's insisting. "Make those lists, then find something fun to do. Do you want me to send you a list of Rhys's favorite shows? Or you could bake cookies. And I'll call you back with my plan later. I need to talk to some people, and if I wake them up now, they'll be grumpy."

Alarm races through me. "What people?" I don't need the world knowing my business.

"Just us," he promises. "Dustin. Sophie. My friend Hagen—have you met him? Don't worry, Ronan. It's going to be fine." He ends the call before I can reply.

I stare at the phone, chewing on my lip. I trust Fabian, but… Sighing, I toss back the covers and get up. Does it even matter? It's not like anything he suggests is going to make things worse.

And he's right. A day away from the cave will let me recharge. Not that I really need—

No. I'm recharging. I'm going to shower because it feels good, even though, since Brandt showed me how to use magic to keep clean, I haven't *needed* to wash. But right now, I want something that feels good. And then I'm going to make those lists Fabian suggested. I think Garrett and Cam might like me? Or at least not dislike me. And Arne is always friendly, now that I'm at the pub so often. I can always buy his friendship.

And then… well… I guess I could make cookies. Or maybe I could try something new, something a bit challenging? I watched Kethe make croissants once. I bet that would distract me.

With a plan set, I square my shoulders and prepare to face the day.

CHAPTER SIX

Zac

I'm a habitually early riser, but even I have to admit that there's something nice about occasionally lying in bed on a Sunday morning and just… being.

Not that I'll do it for very long. I've been awake for twenty minutes now, and that's pretty much my limit. There's a big, wide world out there, and as comfortable as my bed is, I get restless being here when I could be doing something.

So… plans for a lazy Sunday, since I have an unexpected day off. Number one should be trying to come up with a reason for having a day off that'll satisfy Grandmother. On the other hand, nothing's likely to satisfy her, so I may as well just tell her I was sick of being stuck in the cave with Ronan.

Guilt pangs through me. I can't do that, especially not after what I promised my cousins last night. I need to at least *try* to be nicer to Ronan, and that includes not making mean comments about him to others. So I'll just remind Grandmother that slavery is illegal and that Ronan and I decided two days off per week were necessary. She doesn't really like him that much, so I doubt she'll speak with him long enough to find out that the decision was mine.

Okay, that's settled. Hopefully someone else in the family will do something stupid today and I'll be able to fly under the radar at dinner.

So I'll get up, work out in the home gym we've got set up downstairs, and read the paper while I have a leisurely breakfast—which I bet I can probably get Garrett to cook, if I ask nicely. And then I might go for a walk, maybe see if my little cousins want to go skating on the temporary ice rink Zoe set up. That and the snow village aren't going to be around for too much longer—maybe a month or a little more—so we may as well enjoy them while we can. The snowfall is already starting to ease up, and despite Cam's mutterings about the cold, the temperature's been edging a little higher lately. We'll still get snow into May, maybe the occasional overnight flurry in early June, but it won't be sticking around like it does now. Spring is in the air.

With a plan firmly set, I throw back the covers and get up, stretching my arms over my head. I yank on a pair of sweatpants and my running shoes, then wander downstairs.

"Morning, Zac. You're up late today." Garrett doesn't look up from the paper he's reading. I'd stake my life on the fact that he gave Asher big pleading eyes this morning, and my cousin went to Zurich to get it... and then went back to bed. Saves me having to go get my own later.

"Day off," I explain. "I decided to be lazy."

"Good call." He puts the paper down and meets my gaze, his eyes searching. "Listen, about last night—"

I hold up a hand. "It's fine, Garrett. And I promise I'll be nicer to Ronan."

Garrett nods slowly but doesn't look away. "I appreciate that, but I really just wanted to remind you that if you need someone to talk to, we're all here. We've been worried about you."

"Thank you." I don't know what else to say.

"And if you really don't want me and Cam to find a guy for you, we can hold off for a while. Even if we would be better at it than Damaris." His face is solemn, but there's a tiny twinkle in his eye that makes me laugh.

"I can find my own guys, thanks." Although it *has* been a while. Maybe next weekend I should get away from the village, go somewhere with a lot of nightlife and guys looking for a little no-strings fun. Do I want a relationship? Someone to give a shit about me and snuggle up with every night? Of course I do. I'm not a kid anymore, and I'm the homebody type. But I don't want a parade of guys shoved under my nose like Grandmother did with Asher before he met Garrett. When the right guy comes along, I'll know.

Garrett nods, though I'm pretty sure he's bullshitting me and he and Cam will continue their plotting. Lucky for me, it's not that easy for them to throw men in my path up here in the middle of nowhere, cut off from the rest of the world like we are. "Okay, we'll leave it with you." His overly cheery tone just confirms my suspicions. "Hey, do you have a second to look at something for me? I've been trying to come up with plans for the garden at the new house, and Asher said you're the one to ask for tips."

I shrug and join him at the table. "Sure. What do you have in mind?" I'd almost forgotten that when the ground finally thaws, Asher and Garrett will begin construction on their new house. There's a very limited amount of time to get buildings from excavation to weatherproof up here, but after that, the interior work can be done at a more leisurely pace. Even so, it's likely they'll be moving out before the end of the year. Micah's already all but living with Cam, and the thought of being alone here is… not fun.

Shaking that off, I turn my attention to Garrett's ideas. The garden's definitely not going to happen this year, but I can understand him being excited and wanting to plan ahead. I love that he's committed to using native flora too. He also has vague notions of a rock garden, something that can be made to look interesting even outside the growing season, when nearly everything is covered in snow. Rocks and plants are kind of my thing, and I try not to get too excited as we discuss options.

There are worse ways to spend a Sunday morning.

ᔑᒲ

IT'S LATER than I planned when I set out to collect Chloe and Isaac from their respective homes. My aunts and uncles were thrilled by my offer to take the little ones skating and for lunch. I'm looking forward to it—I love being outdoors, and the kids are always fun. Mostly.

I could have teleported to my uncle's house, but the day is nice, Zoe and the snowplow crew have already been through the streets, and why teleport when I can walk? It's not far.

My steps slow as I approach the house Ronan's staying in, guilt weighing on me again. I was going to wait until tomorrow morning to apologize to him, but maybe it's best to do it now? Get it off my chest, clear the air, and we can begin the new week with a fresh start.

Resolved, I turn up the pathway to the front door. Not all of them are cleared of snow, but the houses with non-demons living in them are on the crew's list, since they don't have a way to leave their homes otherwise.

I knock on Ronan's front door and wait. From my

limited understanding of dragons, they have similar sensory abilities to other shifters, so he probably knows it's me. Maybe he'll decide not to open the door.

That would be bad. It would mean I have a *lot* of groveling to do.

To my relief, I hear quiet footsteps approach the door, and then it opens. Ronan gazes at me steadily. He's wearing the same thing he does most days—jeans and a sweater—but there's a streak of white across his brow. Is that flour?

Come to think, I can smell something baking. Barely, though, like it's just gone into the oven. Is he a baker? I didn't know that about him. If I could be sure he wouldn't sock me for it, I'd wipe away that flour and tease him about it. It's endearing.

"Can I help you?" he asks politely. His face is blank. Okay, so it doesn't seem likely he's going to invite me in. Flour wiping is definitely out. That's fine—I get it.

"I came to apologize," I say bluntly. "What I said to you yesterday, in the cave—it was uncalled for and completely unacceptable. You didn't deserve that, and I'm sorry."

For a second, his pretty mouth trembles. Panic strikes —is he going to cry? I'm not equipped to deal with that!

But in the next moment, he regains control. His expression even relaxes a little as he nods. "Thank you, Zac. I appreciate the apology—and accept it. I—" His gaze darts down to his feet and then back up to meet mine, and for some reason, I find myself noticing how very deep a shade of brown they are. "I know I didn't make the best start here in Hortplatz. There are… I have… That is—"

I hold up a hand. "You don't need to explain to me. I haven't been my best self lately either, and unfortunately, you've been getting the worst of that. I promise I'll do better going forward." I extend my gloved hand. It's harder to do than I thought it would be; even though I know Ronan's not to blame for the frustrations in my life right now, part of me really doesn't want to let go of such a handy scapegoat.

He looks at my hand, then shakes it firmly. His ungloved hand is as big as mine, though he's not quite as tall or built as me. But then, he's a dragon, not a demon.

"I'll do better too." It has a ring of determination to it that reminds me he really has been trying to make things up to the people he offended.

I muster a smile. "Okay. Well, I have babysitting duty for my cousins. I'll see you tomorrow."

He nods, smiling back. It only looks a little forced, and still makes his face so much more attractive. "Tomorrow."

I step back and turn away as he closes the door. That wasn't so bad. At least he wasn't a dick about it—he could have refused my apology and told me where to get off.

Or worse, made a complaint about my behavior. This is an inter-government project that's going to benefit Hort-platz in a huge way. If something I did or said caused trouble… well, it's safe to say Grandmother's rampage would be terrifying. I wouldn't have to worry about her match-making me so much as murdering me.

Whistling in an attempt to dispel the nasty thought—it's all good, Ronan accepted my apology—I continue down the street and then cross to my uncle's house. Isaac's little face is plastered to one of the front windows, and he waves excitedly at me, then disappears. I guess he's eager to be going.

The front door is thrown open just as I reach the path. This one hasn't been shoveled today, but Uncle Hal must have done it in the past few days, because the snow's only about a foot deep. I stomp and shuffle my way through it to get to where Isaac is bouncing in the doorway.

"Zac! *Finally*," he shouts, and I grin. "You took forever. Why did you stop at Ronan's house? Is he coming with us?" His eyes widen. "Do dragons like ice-skating?"

Fighting the urge to laugh, I say, "I'm sure some dragons do, and some don't, just the same as demons. He's not coming with us, though. I just needed to talk to him about something for a minute. Were you spying from the window?"

He huffs at me. "It's not spying. I was watching for you. It's only spying if you try not to let anyone see you." The earnest tone of his lecture warns me to be careful of watching eyes in future—it seems Isaac's been caught spying before and has learned how to talk himself out of trouble.

"Uh-huh. Come on, let me in so we can grab your stuff and go get Chloe."

He races down the hall, shouting for his mom, and I step inside and close the door behind me. This is going to be a good day.

CHAPTER SEVEN

Ronan

TEN MINUTES after Zac's gone, I'm still thinking about his apology. It was… nice of him. Yes, what he said to me yesterday was out of line, but not everybody would not only admit that, but show genuine repentance. And he could have waited until tomorrow—instead, he went out of his way to visit. Maybe I should add him to the list Fabian told me to write. We don't have to be friends, but we can probably do better than spending all day, every day alone together in a cave and not speaking.

I really want to be his friend, though. And have him smile at me all the time.

I sigh and reach for the notepad and pen in the middle of the table, where I shoved them in a pique of frustration earlier. Making those lists wasn't easy. I have one each for Garrett, Cam, and Arne, and they're… not exactly long. I don't know much about anyone here because I haven't made any effort to get to know them—not them personally. And now I have to make another one.

Painstakingly, I write Zac's name at the top of a page. Not every dragon and elf bothered to learn how to write by hand, what with computers and tablets and smart-phones being the norm in many countries. It was easier, Fabian told me, for them to learn to recognize typed print and use devices than to master the art of handwriting. It's an undeniable fact, making a pencil or pen shape the letters the way they should look—without using magic to assist—is *hard*. But I considered learning how to be part of my atonement. If things had gone the way *he* planned, many elements of Earth's culture, including handwriting, could have been eradicated. I owe it to the horror of what might have been to carry on what many locals already consider to be a dying art.

Now… what do I know about Zac?

I tap my pen against my lip, the way I saw an actor do in a movie once. It doesn't help. Okay. Think. He's… moody.

No, I can't put that down. Everybody has moods, including me. What else?

He's intelligent—I've seen the periodicals and journals he reads, and they're not lightweight stuff. They're also mostly about science—geology. Botany. Animals.

I write all that down.

He's the town ranger—I can't remember who told me that, but I remember thinking how little comfort it would bring to know that if I got lost in the wilderness, the person in charge of the search would be the one who despised me most. So I suppose he's an outdoorsman. That first time I visited the cave, the others deferred to him on matters of safety. He's the authority when it comes to all of that.

The children love him. He mentioned babysitting duty, but I've seen him around town with little ones clustered around or trailing after him like ducklings.

Speaking of seeing him in town… he's athletic—if you can call snowball fights a form of athleticism. And he's popular. People are always hailing him with big smiles wherever he goes.

I push aside a pang of bitter jealousy. I might not ever be able to have that level of liking and acceptance, but I can build a degree of it.

The oven timer for my croissants buzzes at exactly the same time the doorbell rings. I freeze. Who could that be? Zac, back to tell me he's changed his mind?

Shaking the foolish thought aside, I reach out with my senses as I grab an oven mitt to rescue my croissants. They smell ready, and I don't want to risk them burning while I open the door to… Is that a sorcerer?

My memory fills in the blanks a moment later. It's Zoe, the sorcerer who can do amazing things with snow and ice. I've only met her once, but she was friendly enough and has a lovely smile. I'm not sure what she's doing here, but I doubt it's bad.

Setting the tray on a cooling rack, I close the oven and head toward the front door just as the bell rings again. "I'm coming!" I call, then wonder why I bothered. It just seemed the thing to do.

It's only when I reach for the knob that I realize I'm still wearing the oven mitt. Sighing, I pull it off and open the door.

The tall blonde woman standing on my front step smiles brightly, her cheeks pink from the cold. "Hi! I don't know if you remember me—I'm Zoe?"

I smile back. I can't help it—she looks happy. "Yes, of course. It's good to see you again."

"I'm sorry to interrupt your day off, but I've been—" She stops abruptly and sniffs the air. Her eyes drop to the oven mitt in my hand. "Is that heavenly aroma by any chance coming from your kitchen, and if so, what would it take for me to talk you into sharing some of it with me? A foot rub? Diamonds? A thirty-foot-high snow statue of you?"

A laugh bursts from me, and I stand back, holding the door wide. "Come in. I made too many just for me anyway." I mentally pat myself on the back for sounding so normal when on the inside, I'm screaming with excitement. A visitor who seems to want to spend time with me? Even if it is just for baked goods, this is positive. This is an opportunity to make a connection here in the village. Sure, Zoe's also a newcomer and technically an "outsider," but from everything I've heard, she's made a lot of friends and plans to stay indefinitely.

Zoe walks past me into the house, still sniffing appreciatively.

"Kitchen's down the hall," I tell her, then wonder if I should have shown her into the living room instead. I'm not used to having visitors—never have been. Even before I came to Earth, people didn't so much visit as check up on me.

She doesn't seem offended or fazed, though, stripping off her gloves and hat as I follow her to the kitchen. "Yep, this is definitely the source of that incredible smell. Croissants? Did you make them from scratch, or somehow convince Griff at the supermarket to stock the readymade ones?"

"He'd never do that—he's got a crush on Greta from the bakery," I say automatically, then freeze. "I-I mean… that's just a guess. Nobody said anything to me." Have I ruined this already?

To my relief, Zoe strips off her coat and lays it on the back of a chair with her other outer garments, then sits in the one beside it. "Don't worry, I won't tell. I kinda thought the same. I've been asking him for months to get me some of that American canned dough, at the very least, but he refuses. He never says no to anything else I ask for, so him being sweet on Greta and not wanting to get on her bad side makes sense."

Relieved, I pile the hot croissants on a big plate and bring it to the table. "Jam? Or honey? I don't have anything else, I'm afraid." I was lucky to have enough butter on hand to even make the dough.

She nabs one from the top of the pile. "First one needs to be plain, to get the full experience. Then I'll go from there." She winks at me, and I'm completely charmed.

"Can I get you some tea? I don't have coffee, I'm sorry. But there's water and juice." Like most dragons, after some experimentation, I found that I prefer tea for everyday drinking and reserve coffee for the frothy, milky, flavored concoctions I can get at specialty cafés. Finding I had that in common with my brethren was one of the first things, foolish as it was, that made me feel like a true dragon.

I was sure a hoard would be the clincher, but I'm still waiting for that.

"Tea would be great. Thank you. I swear, I didn't mean to barge in on your day off. Well," she smiles ruefully, "obviously I did after I invited myself in. But the reason I stopped by was to ask if you wanted to get a drink sometime." She bites into the croissant and moans. "Holy crap, this is amazing."

I'm glad for her distraction, because every single thing I've learned about Earth culture in regard to interpersonal relationships is currently streaming through my mind. Did she mean a friendly, welcome-to-town drink, or is this a more personal request?

The kettle is boiling already, probably because it was still warm from earlier, and I carefully spoon the tea leaves into the pot and pour in the water.

"I could live on these croissants, Ronan, seriously.

You're a great baker. So anyway, I barely got to speak to you when you first arrived, and you've been spending so much time in the cave, it didn't seem right to bother you at night, after such long days. But I know how weird it can be trying to settle in here, surrounded by almost only demons, and I thought you might find it handy to have a friend who's been there, done that." She half raises one hand while shoving the last of the croissant into her mouth. "That's me," she says through the crumbs.

Relief floods me so hard, my knees weaken. Friend. I can do that. In fact, I need to do that. This... this is like one of those miracles humans are so fond of. I carry the teapot to the table and go back for mugs, milk, and sugar, then slide into my chair. "I would love that." I'm sure she notices how emphatic I am, but I can't help it.

"Great!" She nabs another croissant, this time breaking it open and drizzling honey over it. "In the spirit of our newfound friendship, I'm going to be honest with you and say I know you've had a rocky start with some of the villagers."

I wince, wishing the tea had steeped enough already. Pouring it would be a great distraction. But Brandt's partner, Percy, was very firm when he taught me the proper way to make tea. *Don't rush it—the perfect cup needs time.*"

"I don't think it's a secret," I confess. Her smile turns sympathetic.

"They feel better about you now, though. There are only a few who are still wary... of the ones who know you, I mean. The population here is small, but a thousand people is still a lot to meet in just a month. How are you finding the weather? Is the cold getting to you?"

I shake my head, checking the pot and finding the tea is finally ready. "Oh, no. Dragons can self-regulate body temperature, so once I got used to the conditions, there was no problem." It had taken me a day or so to get my magic to recognize the new temperature ranges and adjust automatically, rather than me having to consciously maintain it, but since then, I haven't even noticed the cold. I only wear winter gear outdoors so I won't stand out.

I'm so busy pouring our tea that it takes me a moment to realize Zoe is staring at me with her mouth open, hand frozen midair with a piece of croissant in it. Honey is dripping over her fingers.

"Uh, Zoe?" I gesture to her hand. She blinks, looks, then ducks her head and licks the honey away. I slide her mug over to her. "Milk and sugar?"

"Nuh-uh. No way are you going to drop a bombshell like that and then be all, how do you like your tea. Nope. You, mister… you're like the *perfect* friend for me. We can play in the snow all day long and you'd never whine about being cold!"

I'm not sure how to respond to that, so I think we're both surprised when I say, "I've never played in the snow before."

"That's gonna change," she promises, then, to my absolute horror, she taps the notebook lying beside her. "What's this?"

Too late, I realize I should have moved it—at least over to my side of the table. I can't even snatch it away from her, not when she's already got her hand on it.

"I—" Words fail me, and my face gets hot.

"Zachary? Who… oh, you mean Zac. Yeah, he *is* intelligent." She reads the rest of the list silently, then picks up my pen and adds something. Before I can ask what, she's flipping back to the previous pages.

I bury my face in my hands.

"Ronan?" Her voice is gentle, *almost* tempting me to peek between my fingers. "What is this?"

I suck in a deep breath and lower my hands. She doesn't look mad or like she thinks I'm weird.

"It's… I'm not good with people. At making friends." I wonder briefly if I should use Fabian's sex analogy but decide it might be best not to. "Fabian—did you meet him?" She nods. "He said he could help me make better connections here. He's got this plan he hasn't told me about yet, but in the meantime, that was my homework." I gesture to the notepad. "He wanted me to think of people who could maybe get along with me and make a list of what I know about them."

"Oh, honey." Despite the words, her smile is kind, not pitying. "I can't pretend to know what it's like to be shy, because I'm not—not even close—but my sister's bestie can't even look people in the eye without blushing." She reaches out and pats my hand. "Don't worry—me and Fabian, we can help you meet people. I'm happy to be a safe person for you here."

The sheer weight of feeling that crashes through me leaves me incapable of speech, but Zoe doesn't seem to need an answer. She's looking back down at the notepad. "You've made a great start here," she adds. "Cam likes you —he's the one who called to tell me you had today off. He knew I'd been wanting to introduce myself properly. And trust me, he's never met a stranger, so he's a great ally to have. Garrett, too—he's yelled at Zac a bunch already for giving you a hard time." She winces. "Sorry, but you have to know Zac isn't your greatest fan. I'm kinda surprised you made a list for him."

"I didn't at first," I start, then find myself telling her everything—about how Zachary and I barely speak, the way our few verbal exchanges tend to be snide. I skip over what he said yesterday—no need to bring that up—but I explain the way he apologized today. "I thought that since he seems open to the idea of starting over, it might be good to be prepared."

She nods slowly, then jumps to her feet. There's an expression on her face I'm not quite sure how to interpret. "Come on… let's go out. It's a nice day; there's plenty of people in the snow village. This is a great opportunity for you to be social, and I swear, I won't leave your side."

Reflexively, I begin to protest, but… she's right. "Okay."

"Great!" She grins. "I just need to pee first."

I direct her to the bathroom, then busy myself tidying away the dishes and food. I lift the notepad to wipe the tabletop, and my eye catches on what she wrote on Zachary's page.

Single—gay—hot as fuck.

CHAPTER EIGHT

Zac

FAMILY DINNER TONIGHT IS QUIET.

Too quiet.

Someone-fucked-up-and-Grandmother's-about-to-go-ballistic quiet.

Even the kids have noticed and are diligently working their way through their food with their heads down. I exchange a look with Asher, then Micah. This is… not good.

"So," Aunt Hilda attempts gamely, "tell us how skating was today, kids."

Isaac lifts his gaze, flicks it around the table, then says, "I don't want to," before going back to his potatoes. A hysterical bubble of laughter catches in my throat.

Chloe, older and braver, chimes in with, "It was good." But there are limits to even her courage.

I'm trying to catch my mother's eye—maybe she can steer us in the right direction; she and Grandmother are two peas in a pod—when Cam blithely makes a fatal mistake.

He makes a second attempt to get the conversation going.

And, unfortunately, he drags me right into the middle of the shitstorm.

"Has Zac spoken to any of you about his idea for a ski resort?" he asks, spearing some green beans. Does he… not notice the tension in the room? "I think it could be a real winner… and I've never been skiing before. Micah promised to take me."

I glare at Micah, begging him to do something.

Uncle Hal clears his throat, steals a glance at Grandmother's stony face, and bravely tries to support his potential future son-in-law. "A ski resort? I thought it was too steep around here for anything like that."

Cam shakes his head, then nods. "Oh, it is, mostly, but there's an area that could be used. I think it would have been too expensive and not worth it when people couldn't get up here year-round, but now that Garrett's planning to implement regular transportation, it could be worth it. Right, Zac? Tell them what you were thinking. Micah, stop that. If you need more room for your leg, move your chair. There's no need to jostle me."

Micah closes his eyes in frustration and despair, and I steel myself. "It's not going to happen," I say quietly. "My plans have been shelved."

Cam frowns. "But why?"

Garrett, whose face has been twisted with indecision for the last few minutes, adds, "Asher said you'd mentioned that—shelving the plans. Is the problem to do with the expenses? Because I think we—"

"The problem," Grandmother breaks in, her voice so cold that I need to stop myself from shivering, "is that Zachary spends so much time on his foolish dreams that he allows himself to damage our community and what we're trying to build here."

I can almost feel the blood draining from my face. Me? It's me she's mad at? *Why?* I haven't done anything since my attempted pitch for the resort, and she wasn't this angry at the time.

But her gimlet gaze is drilling into me now, and I have no choice but to face this. "I'm not sure what you mean. I would never do anything to damage our community. And"—might as well be hanged for a sheep as for a lamb—"the ski resort would attract people to the community who aren't interested in the museum, as well as providing accommodation to support academics in the summer. I want to help what we're building." I stop abruptly. Asher's giving me a wide-eyed "you got balls, but stop if you wanna keep them" look.

"Oh?" Grandmother's brow rises, and sweat breaks out down my spine. She wouldn't kill me. She loves me. I'm her grandson. She's never killed a relative.

We think.

Has anyone ever confirmed that?

Too late now.

"Well, Zachary, if indeed you want to help what we're building, perhaps you could explain to us all why you've so severely insulted the dragon representative?"

I try to keep my breathing steady. This is about Ronan? Seriously? Just when I've resolved to be nice to him, *now* she wants to yell at me about rudeness?

And since when has she cared that much about rudeness anyway?

"I admit I've been less than welcoming to Ronan," I say carefully. "Asher and Micah have already reminded me that I owe him respect and hospitality. I'll be making more of an effort in future."

She scoffs. "As if I care that you're grouchy and pigheaded! It's not as though his manner has been all that genteel. No, I'm referring to the outright, unforgiveable insult you gave him yesterday. When you accused him of, how did you put it? *Sulking in the dark*, I believe it was. You suggested that he might be hiding instead of working and told him not to waste your time!"

There are quiet gasps around the table, shocked faces turning toward me. I deserve that. I know I do. Here's the thing, though…

How did she know?

There were only two people in the cave when that happened: Me. And Ronan.

I know I didn't tell anyone what I said. I was too ashamed of myself to repeat it, even to my cousins. Which means Ronan must have made a complaint.

Hot anger rushes through me, obliterating all reason. How fucking dare he have looked me in the eye this morning when he'd—

Wait. I take a deep breath, trying to think. Everyone's eyes are on me. Grandmother's glare is scrambling my wits. But something's not right here.

Ronan and I aren't friends. We're not even friendly. Maybe he's trying now, and maybe when I get to know him, he'll turn out to be a great guy, but right now, today, that's not how I feel. But. *But.* When I left his house this morning, I was sure we were both going to try to get along better. He was wary when he opened the door—not like someone who was expecting me to come and apologize. And if he'd officially complained yesterday, there's no way in hell I wouldn't have heard about it before now. I saw three members of the village council while I was out today, and they were just as friendly and casual as ever.

Which means either Ronan didn't make an official

complaint, just tattled on me to Grandmother—which seems unlikely, since he barely knows her—or he waited until this afternoon, after he'd accepted my apology and we'd agreed to a truce, to make his complaint, thereby stabbing me in the back.

This seems the most obvious option. He might not even see it as a betrayal, given how difficult I've made things for him. It's just… remembering his face when he thanked me for apologizing and admitted he was trying harder, I can't see him doing that. He seemed, if not happy, then at least resolved to start over. I don't believe he looked at me so hopefully and then just a few hours later made a complaint about something I'd already apologized for.

So… how does Grandmother know?

Did Ronan tell someone else? Not a formal complaint, just a comment to a friend? That's possible, and I wouldn't blame him for it. But… I didn't think he had friends like that here. Even if he did, I can't think of anyone in town who wouldn't come and yell at me first before tattling on me to Grandmother. If it was another dragon or a friend from home… would they make a complaint on his behalf without even telling him? Because for some reason I don't understand, I have this unshakable belief that if he'd known, he would have called and warned me.

I look Grandmother dead in the eye. "How did you know about that?"

"Zac," my mother begins angrily, "that's not the most important part here."

I don't look her way; I know what I'll see. Fury and disappointment. My mom loves me, completely and without any reservations. But she's never been okay with bad manners, and she already told me once in the past few weeks to smarten up my attitude.

"Grandmother? How did you know?" I repeat.

"Nothing happens in Hortplatz that I don't know about," she snaps. "You think I don't know how you joke about that?"

"We do," I agree. I'm pretty sure Micah has stopped breathing. "But this didn't happen in Hortplatz. This happened in the cave."

"You can't blame Ronan for this," Uncle Sol protests. "Zac, I thought better of you. He had the right to protest you saying that to him."

I nod. I'm suddenly absolutely certain of what happened, and it sends cold chills through me that she would do this. "I agree. He had the right. I don't blame Ronan at all for what happened yesterday. I was wrong to say what I did, and I regretted it. But I find it difficult to believe that he would complain to Grandmother about what I said and then *not* follow up after I went to see him this morning and apologized."

Dead silence. Grandmother's face is stone.

"You apologized?" Mom sounds cautious.

"Sincerely and unreservedly. I was wrong. My attitude has been poor, and I took it out on him more than once—but yesterday I crossed the line. He accepted my apology, and we agreed to a truce." I don't look away from Grandmother. "Ronan and I aren't friends, and I haven't thought highly of him since we met, but I don't believe he would have looked me in the eye and lied about wanting to get along better. I don't believe he said anything about what happened yesterday. So how did you know, Grandmother?"

Her nostrils flare, and it's obvious enough that even a non-demon would have noticed. "Since you have apologized, we will put this behind us. But if you ever disgrace this family like that—"

"How did you know?" I'm not letting her off the hook that easy. "Have you bugged the cave?"

Into the heavy silence that follows, Aunt Hilda clears her throat. "Chloe, Isaac, you're excused." It's a testament to the mood in the room that neither child says a word—they just push back their chairs and flee.

Grandmother says nothing.

"Where else have you bugged?" She knows everything that happens in Hortplatz—we joke about it, because it seems so true. We always thought that was just because she's a busybody and people tell her things, but...

"Have you bugged *us*? Do you invade every second of our lives?"

That finally gets a reaction. "Don't be ridiculous," she snaps. "This melodrama doesn't suit you, Zachary."

"I'm not the one planting bugs like I'm in an espionage thriller," I retort. "Since it never occurred to me you might be spying on us all electronically, I have some questions now that I know you are."

"I'm not spying on you. The devices in the cave were placed for security purposes. There are a great many valuables in that vault."

"So the village council knows they're there? And surely Garrett—he's in charge of the project, after all. He knows all about it?" I challenge. I know he doesn't. He would have mentioned it.

She gives her head a sharp shake. "It was a unilateral decision. In matters of security, the more people who know, the bigger the chance of a leak."

I can't argue the logic of that statement. Fortunately, I don't have to.

"Damaris," Garrett begins firmly. His face is set, and I know he hates having to face her down. "Given that I am, in fact, in charge of the project—which is something *you* insisted on—I'm going to have to demand that you give me the details of any and all security measures you've taken. We can discuss it after dinner."

Grandmother looks like she wants to argue, but she's on shaky ground and knows it. She nods once.

"Um…" Cam half raises his hand. "Can I just ask… when was the bug put in the cave?"

We all look to Grandmother. "When the satellite connection was installed," she says stiffly. "It would have been useless before then."

"Oh. Phew." Cam grins at Micah, who looks like he wants to be anywhere but here, and nobody at the table has any doubt that they *did things* in the cave while Cam was solving the puzzle. I make a mental note to ask Micah which surfaces I need to sanitize.

Dinner breaks up then—nobody has much of an appetite after all that. I slip away while Garrett's talking to Grandmother, hoping to avoid any further confrontation tonight.

The only good thing that happened was not having to listen to Grandmother shoot down the ski resort project—again—but this time in front of everyone who loves me.

CHAPTER NINE

Ronan

WHEN I LET myself into my borrowed house that evening, I'm humming. *Humming.* I can't remember the last time I hummed. I think I was small—and then Nurse told me humming was a common kind of thing to do, and I should stop.

I don't have to worry about that anymore, though, and humming is *delightful.* I may even sing one day soon.

I'm happy, and I'm not sure if I've ever been happy before. Not like this, anyway. I used to think I was happy, as a child, but with hindsight and perspective, I can see that my happiness was always earned. I would be happy when I was praised for doing something correctly or if I'd done something that pleased somebody else. I can't remember ever being happy simply because I had a good time in good company, like today.

I strip off my outer garments, which Zoe teased me about wearing, now that she knows I don't need them, and leave them on an armchair. I'll tidy them away later—for now, the couch is calling, and I flop onto it gratefully.

Being happy is tiring. But it's a good tired—I'll gladly be this tired forever.

Zoe hustled me out of the house this morning, and since then, my day has been a whirlwind. She seems to know nearly everyone in the village, and they like her. To be fair, it's hard not to like Zoe—she has this contagious energy that just makes you want to smile. She took me to the snow village first, and even though I've been there before, it was different with her. Partly because she built it and could point out all the little details and hidey-holes I'd missed, but also because she talks to *everyone*. If she's not calling out to them, they're coming up to her. And she stuck to her promise not to leave my side—all day, she was saying, "Have you met Ronan? He's my new dragon bestie," or "You would *not* believe how good his croissants are," and including me in conversations. At first I felt awkward, but it got easier and easier when people were so nice. I spent the afternoon actually talking to people and getting to know them. Surprisingly few people asked me about being a dragon—they were more interested in where I'd been living, what work I do, and how things are going in the cave. One man wanted to know about my home-world, but his wife shushed him and said, "You don't need to answer that. We had to leave our home when we came here, and sometimes it still hurts to remember."

I was grateful for her intercession, because the truth is, I don't have a lot of firsthand information about the world I was born on. My whole life was spent in a series of compounds, supposedly for my safety. I've heard others talk about the tréghel trees and the plains and mountain ranges, about oceans so deep the water goes from palest pink to black. But I never saw them, and now I never can.

Then Zoe decided we should have dinner at the pub,

and we trooped over there to find it already half full of people who'd had the same idea. I've eaten at the pub so many times, but this time when Arne hailed me and gestured to an open seat at the bar, Zoe waved him off and dragged me to a table.

A table.

I ate at a table. With a friend.

People kept stopping by to say hello, and not just to Zoe! Some of them came over to say hi to me, regulars that I see here all the time. One family was celebrating a birthday and offered everyone slices from the huge cake they'd brought, and Arne decided since it was a birthday party, we should have some dancing. I don't know where the fiddle came from or who the person playing it was, but the music was fun. I even danced a little. I'm sure I looked like a fool, but nobody laughed at me.

It's been a great day. Before we parted ways, Zoe suggested we plan a movie night for next weekend with Cam and Garrett. She hinted about inviting Asher and Micah too, but if we do that, we can't leave Zachary out, right? Those three are close. I'd feel bad. And despite our agreement to get along better, I'm not sure if I'm ready to socialize with him. I want to see how this week goes first.

Truthfully, I'm not sure I'd be comfortable socializing with Asher or Micah, either. Especially Asher, after he witnessed the humiliating moment when Garrett asked if I might be speciesist. I could tell Garrett was sympathetic, but Asher, with his demon face, was harder to read.

So I committed to a movie night, but we've left the guest list open to negotiation for now. A movie night! With a friend! And other people who might become friends.

My phone rings, and I answer it without even looking at the screen. "Hello?"

There's a tiny pause. "You sound happy," Fabian says. "Have you been jerking off?"

"Fabian!" someone else exclaims, and I recognize the voice as Sophie, the dragon healer. "You're not supposed to *ask* stuff like that."

"How else is he going to find out the answer?" another voice asks. I don't recognize this one. Just how many people are on this call?

"He needs to be subtle," Dustin, Brandt's grandson, says authoritatively.

There's a moment of doubting silence. "How would I subtly ask something like that?" Fabian asks.

Dustin clears his throat and inquires, with studied casualness, "So, Ronan, have you had a good day? What have you been up to?"

My grin is so wide, I think my face might crack. "I've had a great day, thank you, Dustin." I stop there and let them wait. I never knew teasing people could be so much fun.

Surprisingly, it's Sophie who cracks first. "What did you do?"

I laugh. "Not jerk off." My cheeks get hot even saying the words. It's not that I don't do it—of course I do. But I don't talk about it. Ever. To anyone.

"Did someone else jerk you off?" the unknown person asks. "Because otherwise, this conversation is getting boring really fast, and I've got a hot vampire boyfriend I could probably convince to give me a blowjob."

My face feels like fire now, and I'm glad none of them can see me. "I don't want to be rude, but who are you?"

"Oh, sorry! I meant to make introductions. My bad," Fabian announces. "Ronan, this is Hagen. He's a friend who's really good at pissing people off and getting them to like him anyway. I thought he could be helpful."

I know that should be reassuring, given my situation, but I'm not sure it is. "Things have changed a little since this morning," I inform him. "I still need help, though," I add quickly. For all I know, today was an anomaly, and I'll be back to lonely, desperate misery tomorrow.

"That's what we're here for," Dustin explains proudly. "We're your on-call support team. Fabian's going to set up a group chat so you can ask for help anytime you need it. We're still discussing what to call ourselves, though."

"Tonight's call is to introduce the group and make sure everyone has the background info," Fabian adds. "So, spill. What happened today?"

Pleased that these people are willing to help me, even Hagen, who I've never met (though I have heard about him, and if even half the stories are true, I'm not sure I'll want to follow his advice), I tell them everything that happened from the moment I last spoke to Fabian.

"Wow," Sophie says. "This is fantastic!"

I glow with pride. "I had a good day. A happy day."

"You did great," Dustin encourages. "Maybe we should add Zoe to our chat? Fabian, did you meet her?"

"Ummmm," Fabian says. "Yes? Blond sorcerer, right? The one who does all the snow stuff?"

"That's her," I confirm.

"Sure, I met her! She's great. But let's wait before we add her—I want Ronan to get advice from two perspectives. That way, he'll have clearer options to choose from."

I'm not sure if that makes sense. I play the words over in my head, but the others are still talking, and I can't quite pin down what's tripping me up.

"Okay, so you have a friend on the ground who can help," Hagen says. "Sounds like the next hurdle is this Zac guy. What do we know about him?"

"After he apologized, I started making a list about him too, like Fabian said," I blurt. "There's not much on it." And ever since I saw what Zoe added, the whole list is burned into my brain. I tell them all the things I wrote but leave off Zoe's contribution. It's not pertinent to the conversation.

Even if it is true. He's single. From everything I've heard, he's gay. And hot as fuck might, possibly, be an understatement. The first time I saw him, before we'd had any interaction, I found myself wondering how his beard would feel against someone's skin. Mine, to be exact.

"Okay, so this is an easy way to start," Dustin said. "He's outdoorsy and reads a lot of nature magazines? Ask him about the area."

"That's a good one," Sophie agrees. "You went to the snow village today, right? So tell him that and then ask what people do in summer when there's no snow."

"Remember that you can fly," Hagen adds. "People are *always* impressed by that. Tell him you're not that experienced at mountain climbing or whatever, but can he suggest any places worth seeing that you can fly to." He hesitates. "When he likes you more, you can maybe take him flying. But I'd hold off on that until you're sure he won't tell you to land somewhere really abandoned and then murder you."

I blink slowly. "I… I don't think he's going to murder me." Would he? No. Damaris, maybe. "He's the easygoing one in the family… with most people."

"Are you sure? Some of these demons can be kind of intense. I've met Gideon Bailey, and aren't they cousins?"

I've met Gideon Bailey, too, and that's what gives me the certainty to say, "I'm sure." I could easily imagine Gideon murdering me in cold blood—especially when we first met. Zac, on the other hand, even yesterday, when he was so cruel… he would never.

"Let's add a future flying trip to the list, then," Fabian declares. "I agree that it might need to wait until you're actually friends, but in the meantime, I bet you can open a lot of minds by taking someone else up for a flight. Maybe Zoe?"

I think about Zoe's ready-for-adventure personality and love of the cold. "She'd definitely like that. But I don't have a harness." I've never taken anyone up on my back before, but I've seen others do it. While it is *technically* possible for a rider to hold on without any kind of harness, it's difficult and stupidly irresponsible. Wil, who was in charge of my flying lessons, told me that young dragons are drilled repeatedly about never taking a passenger without a harness.

Of course, that doesn't mean it's never done. I've heard stories about people pulling stunts—apparently, shortly after our arrival on Earth, several dragons and hellhounds invented a new sport called firediving. But if I want to make friends and keep them, it seems to me that a harness is the way to go.

"We can get one to you," Dustin assures me. "Right? Hagen, can you ask Caolan to portal it over?"

"Yep. He might ask why, though."

"Wait." Sophie's voice is incredulous. "He might ask you why you want him to take a dragon-riding harness to a dragon?"

There's a momentary pause, then a sheepish Hagen says, "Okay, yeah, I hear it now."

"Hear what?" Fabian asks. "Is there interference on the line?"

I grin. I'd forgotten how much fun Fabian can be just by being himself. Dustin explains, and Fabian makes a pfft sound. "Hagen, if you can't keep up, I'm going to need to reconsider your invitation to join this team. This is serious business. Life or death stuff."

I open my mouth to protest that it's not *that* serious, but Hagen is already solemnly apologizing and vowing to focus more.

"Okay," Fabian continues, "on the primary list, I've got continue friendship with Zoe, including offer to take her flying. Then also go to this movie night and see how you go with… the other people. Who were they, again?"

"Cam and Garrett," I supply automatically. "Wait, there's an actual list? You're writing a list?"

"More than one." The heavy patience in his tone makes me feel like a chastised child. "You've been eating at the pub a few nights a week, too, haven't you? Keep doing that. Let people see you being normal."

I'm not completely sure Fabian, who frequently forgets to put on clothes when he's in research mode and can be found wandering around naked, is the authority on normal. But I let that slide.

"Now, on the Zachary list… I think you need to ease into him."

"That's what he said," Hagen says, and snickers.

Huh? "I don't understand."

"I'll explain it to you later," Dustin says. "It's a joke."

"Start with any kind of conversation at all," Fabian says, and it takes me a second to realize that he's either ignoring the interruption or didn't even notice it. With Fabian, either is possible. "You don't normally talk, right? That's what you said? So ask him what he did on the weekend. It doesn't need to be specific to his interests—just get the dialogue started."

I turn that over in my mind. He did say he was on

babysitting duty today—I could ask how that went. "Okay. I can handle that."

"Don't try too hard," Sophie says gently. "Remember, at this point, any conversation is a good start. If he doesn't seem to want to chat, let it go. Slow and steady will get you there."

"Also what he said," Hagen murmurs. I really need to find out what that means.

"I think we can leave it there for today," Fabian declares. "Ronan, are you feeling more positive than you did before?"

I take a deep breath and consider it. "Yes. I know it won't always be as easy as today, but I think I have a chance now."

"Great! So I'll set up the chat, and whenever you need help, just reach out!"

"Thank you," I tell them all, and with a flurry of good-byes, the call ends. Smiling, I think about maybe watching something on TV. Normally I'd work, but maybe I should try to relax.

My phone chimes, and I glance at the notification.

FABIAN DRACO HAS INVITED YOU TO JOIN THE
CHAT NAME NEEDED.

Did he… did he actually name the chat "Name Needed"? I click into it just as the first message pops up.

FABIAN:

Taking suggestions for the group name! I like Ronan's Heroes, but that might be cultural appropriation from that human TV show. I'm not sure. Dustin, can you ask Rob?

FABIAN:

> Attaching the first two lists for everyone's reference.

As the links to the attachments pop up on my screen, I wonder if asking Fabian for help might not have been the best idea after all.

CHAPTER TEN

Zac

FOR THE FIRST time since I got volunteered to be Ronan's transport-slash-aide-slash-guide, I'm not planning to slog through the snow to knock at his front door this morning. I always did it that way to maintain some distance between us—I guess as a snub. A sign that I don't consider him a safe enough acquaintance to risk teleporting directly into his home. Though since he doesn't know all that much about demons, I can't say how effective it was. Now that I've promised to be civil, I hope he didn't understand what I was doing, because after giving it some thought, I've decided to treat him the same way I did—do—Cam.

So I pull out my phone and text him.

> Is it okay if I teleport into your house this morning to pick you up?

It's a few minutes before he replies.

> Yes, of course. Do I need to do anything?

Guilt slams into me. He's living in a village full of

demons, and nobody's explained to him the function of the teleport rooms? I should have done that. As his liaison, I'm responsible for those details.

> No—did Garrett show you where the teleport room is? Just don't be in there. I'll come at the usual time.

> Okay. I know where it is. I'll see you then. Thank you.

I stare at the screen. What's he thanking me for? Unless he *does* know that me not teleporting into his house was insulting to him, and now he's glad I'm showing trust?

Or it could just be a politeness thing. I've noticed that he's very polite—even when it seemed like he loathed every second of having to be here, he was always courteous. It was in direct contrast to the other dragon who stayed a few days, Fabian, who was friendly but sometimes blunt to the point of rudeness—but in a not-rude way.

"Zac?" Garrett's call has me looking toward the kitchen doorway. He appears there a moment later. "Oh good, you haven't left. I've made a decision about Damaris's little spy devices." His voice and face are grim.

He talked to Grandmother for quite some time last night, and I know it was difficult for him. She's intimidating even when she's feeling kind and benevolent, and last night was not one of those times. Still, according to what Asher reported when they got back, Garrett stood firm in his role as project coordinator and insisted she hand over control of her surveillance in the cave.

She actually did it too.

"Oh?" I ask. I don't for a single second believe that she's really given Garrett full control of everything, and judging by his face right now, neither does he.

"I thought about leaving them in place for additional security, but electronics are too easily hacked. Especially a system like this that needs an external feed out. And…" He hesitates. "I love Damaris, believe it or not. She's my family now. I definitely respect her. But I don't particularly trust her on this. My money is on her having backup devices or a backdoor into the network."

I nod, trying not to grin. Asher married a smart man.

"So Ash and I are going up to the cave this morning to clear out all the bugs and then run a sweep to see if there are any extras. You were at the cave when they installed the signal boosters—did they go into the vault?"

Immediately, I shake my head. "Absolutely not. I kept the door most of the way closed and sat in the gap watching while the workers were there, just like we agreed. The only way a bug would have gotten into the vault is if one of them lobbed it over my head—which I would have noticed."

His shoulders sag with relief. "That's one good thing, at least. Can you distract Ronan until we're done? We don't want anyone else in there in case it interferes with what we're doing. Be late to pick him up or something."

I wince. "I just finished texting him that I'd be there at the usual time."

"Ugh. Well, think of something to delay getting there. We need about an hour, and we're leaving right now."

I look at the wall clock. There's still a half hour or so until I'm due to collect Ronan, so I'd only need to delay him for about thirty minutes. But something about it all sits sourly in my stomach. We *just* agreed to a truce yesterday, and I'm going to start things out by deceiving him?

"What if," I start slowly, and Garrett's expression turns expectant. "What if I… told him?"

For a second, he doesn't get it. "Told him wh— Oh."

"It's just…" I try to get my thoughts together enough to explain, but everything is all tangled up in the guilt I still feel. "It's his privacy that's been invaded. I mean, Grandmother listening in on me reading a magazine, or even on shit I say… I don't like it, but I can tell her that to her face and not cause a diplomatic incident. Plus, my whole life, I've always known that she knows everything."

It's an attempt at a joke, but it falls flat now. Eavesdropping devices are a relatively new invention, but she's always liked technological gadgets. For all we know, she's been using them since they were first invented.

"I just feel like he has the right to know she was listening. And that the whole family knows what I said to him. He… I think I hurt him, Garrett." It costs me to say that. He already knows I apologized, but I still don't like admitting that I was… mean. Spiteful.

Garrett's silent, and I know he's thinking about the ramifications. Which I didn't. Shit.

"Would it affect the agreement?" I ask. "The listening devices being there?"

He grimaces. "If we left them there without informing the village council, CSG, and the DEA, yes. They've each allocated a security liaison to work with me, and those people have full access to any security plans we have in place. Me having secret surveillance would violate that agreement. My options when I found out it already existed were to remove it or tell them about it and give them all access."

Um… "Isn't removing it without telling them it was there a violation of the agreement anyway?"

He looks me dead in the eye. "Yes. But if I tell them what Damaris did…"

I get it now. Garrett's protecting her. The combined governments wouldn't look kindly on her little spy network.

Given her influence and the work she's done for the community over the years, she'd barely get a slap on the wrist, but the humiliation of even that much…

"Dammit," I mutter.

"Yeah."

Nearly two centuries of always, *always* putting family first, always remaining loyal weigh on me now. My whole life has been about protecting the family and our people. About the responsibility we have to those in our compound —the village, now—who aren't as strong, don't have as much wealth. The Bailey family's standing in the community of species—*Grandmother's* standing—has been a stalwart barrier shielding us all. For it to come out that she violated the terms of an inter-government agreement— even if the news was restricted only to those with the highest security clearance—well… that would be a blow.

But on the other hand, I can't shake the feeling that I need to tell Ronan about this. That he deserves to know.

This has to be the worst Monday morning ever.

Swallowing hard, I tell Garrett, "Could you put some kind of preliminary report together? Maybe a message saying there's been a minor security hiccup, it's been handled, and a full report is coming later? Something you can send with thirty seconds' notice just so it's on record that you did report it."

He lets out a slow, shaky sigh. "You're going to tell him."

"I have to. Maybe if I explain, he won't report it. But…" I clench my hands into fists, trying to work out what's going on in my head. "He's trying so hard, Garrett. I know I haven't been good to him, but while he's here, he's ours to protect, and this feels like a betrayal. I told him we'd start over. We called a truce. I can't look him in the eye knowing…" I shake my head.

"No, I get it. I'll type up a text message, leave it in drafts. If it seems like he's going to report it, give me a heads-up." He hesitates. "For what it's worth, I don't think he will."

"Oh?" Hope surges in me.

"You're right; he *is* trying. Yesterday… I don't know if you heard, but Zoe's befriended him. She introduced him to half the village, and last night he was dancing at the pub with everyone else."

"Last night?" I echo. It's not even eight in the morning. "How do you know this already?"

"Zoe messaged me and Cam last night. She wants the three of us and Ronan to have a movie night on Friday. I think he's lonely, Zac. I think he's socially awkward and lonely and probably has other things on his mind, and it's made things a lot harder for him than they need to be. If we—" He takes a deep breath. "If we show some honesty and trust, maybe he'll be inclined to reciprocate."

We both take a second to think about that and hope we're not making a stupid decision. If Ronan is angry enough to report what Grandmother did—if the dragons are so offended that they make a fuss—it's not just this project that's in jeopardy. The relations between governments might become strained as well. Gideon is the current lucifer's boyfriend and very highly placed at CSG in his own right. How will the DEA react to the knowledge that his grandmother was spying on one of their people?

"You and Asher better get going," I manage, looking at the clock again. I somehow have to wait another twenty minutes before I can even go to Ronan's. I'm pretty sure it's going to feel like hours.

"Let me know as soon as you've spoken with him" is all Garrett says in parting.

I sink back in my chair and wait.

The teleport room in Ronan's house is just like all the other teleport rooms Micah designed—small and functional. There is absolutely no excuse to stay in here a second longer.

And yet, it takes me an interminably long time to reach the door. My legs suddenly feel like they weigh a ton.

For fuck's sake, Zac, get over it. He'll either take it well or won't. And if he doesn't, you can go back to being an ass to him.

My inner self gives a heck of a pep talk, but it's wrong. If Ronan doesn't take this well, I'm not going to revert to my old behavior. He's entitled to get upset about being spied on.

I open the door and step into the hallway. "Ronan?"

"I'm here!" he calls, and a second later, appears from the front of the house. "Sorry, I didn't know if I should wait in the hallway or if that wasn't—" He stops, visibly pulling himself together. "Good morning." His smile is tentative—a test of our truce.

I try to make myself smile back, but my face won't respond, and the hopeful light in his eyes begins to fade. *No!* I take a quick step forward. "Good morning. Uh… do you have a moment to talk? There's something you s-should know."

His entire body goes still. "Is my brother…?"

"It's nothing like that," I race to assure him. "I'm sure your brother's fine. This is… It's complicated. And kind of a long story."

He takes a step back. "Perhaps we should sit. Please come this way."

I follow him into the living room. It's just as plainly furnished as it was when we assigned the house to him—if he brought any personal things with him, they're in another room. Choosing an armchair, I sit, put my hands on my knees, and look at him.

Then search vainly for the words to begin.

He waits, and with every passing second, his face closes more and more. I'm losing ground—losing any rapport we might have begun to build. It wasn't much, just a tentative thread, but if I don't speak, it's going to snap.

"I want you to know that I knew nothing about this until last night," I blurt. "I swear it. I'll swear it on anything you want me to. I would never have done this, not to you or anyone. And I didn't know anything about it when I came here yesterday. I meant my apology, I still mean it, and I'd like for us to have a better working… association." I was going to say "relationship," but for some reason, it felt wrong.

His face has paled somewhat, but he only nods.

"Last night at dinner, my grandmother lambasted me for what I said to you on Saturday. I…" It seems pointless to explain my thought process at the time, so I skip to, "I demanded to know how she'd found out, and it eventually came out that she's had electronic surveillance in the cave since the Wi-Fi booster was installed."

His mouth drops open, but I don't stop. "This is a direct violation of the security agreement in place for the project. Garrett and Asher are removing all the devices as I speak and will sweep to ensure there aren't any others." I suck in a deep breath. "We debated whether to tell you, but given the violation of your right to privacy, we decided we couldn't keep it from you." I hesitate. "Right now, the only people who know about this are my family. My grandmother, who was solely responsible. My mother, my uncles and aunts. Asher, Micah, Garrett, Cam. And me. I'm not sure what Grandmother might have observed or listened to from the few days that were recorded, but the only thing everyone else knows is what I said to you on Saturday. *Nobody*," I give the word heavy emphasis, "will ever speak of it. They're all ashamed of my behavior."

He gives his head a quick little shake, almost an automatic movement. "You apologized. We put it behind us."

His words lapse into silence. I don't know what to say. There's nothing I *can* say. The next move is his.

"Garrett and Asher are removing all the devices?" he asks finally.

"Yes," I assure him, then decide to go for broke. "Garrett debated leaving them in place and making them part of the official security procedure, but decided the way they were set up posed a greater risk than anything else."

Ronan's gaze, which had drifted toward the carpet minutes ago, rises to meet mine. "Not to mention that making it part of the official security procedure would mean advising the security representatives from the DEA and CSG of its existence."

My mouth goes dry. "Yes."

He watches me, his face a mask so impenetrable, it could be a demon's. "What happens if I report this to the DEA's security representative—my brother?"

Garrett didn't mention that little tidbit, but it makes sense, given what I know about Steffen Draco. "Officially, this is a violation of the agreement. We can prove that Grandmother acted alone and without the knowledge or support of the village council or anyone on the project team. Grandmother will certainly be asked to resign from the council and removed from any connection to the project. She may face criminal charges, but I don't believe those would stick." I clear my throat. "It's also possible that Garrett would be removed as coordinator and that control of the project would be given to a team made up of government officials from outside the village. I'm not certain what the long-term ramifications are regarding the planned museum and tourism."

He nods slowly. "You said 'officially.' What happens unofficially?"

I didn't think he'd catch that.

"My grandmother... she's an old demon, and she's amassed a lot of influence over the years. Our family already had a lot before she married my grandfather, and together, they pretty much... built an empire. She's... I know she's not an easy person to know. Not even for us, sometimes. But she does do a lot of good for the community. For her, duty to her people is everything. Sometimes she gets so caught up in that, she forgets that people are also individuals, not just a faceless entity. This would do a lot of damage to her reputation, and that could have ripple effects." I leave it there. We don't know exactly what would happen. Speculation isn't going to help.

He nods again, clearly thinking.

Impulsively, I lean forward. "Ronan, you have every right to report this to Steffen. To the DEA. Your privacy was invaded, and the agreement was breached. I'm not here to convince you to do otherwise. We—Garrett and I —thought you had the right to know what happened. And... if you do decide to report this, I ask if you would please give me ten minutes so Garrett can advise the security team first. But if you prefer, you can take my phone now and hold on to it while you call your brother." I make eye contact again. "Whatever happens, I won't blame you. Nobody will."

There's another heavy silence.

"I've never done anything in that cave or the vault except the work I was sent here to do," he says at last. "I've never said anything I'm ashamed of. I will not tolerate being surveilled without my knowledge and consent, not ever again. If Garrett will assure me that all devices have been removed, and that neither Damaris nor any agents of hers will have access to the cave at any time for the duration of my task here, then I see no reason for a report to be made."

I swear, for a second it feels like my heart stops beating in my chest. "She won't," I swear. "Garrett won't let her near the place, and he'll oversee any future visitors himself. They'll all be screened by him." And probably his cousin Alistair and Gideon, though I doubt Garrett will tell them why he wants their help. "You can talk to him about it, but there's no way any of us will let Grandmother jeopardize this for us again."

My phone rings before he can reply. "That's probably Garrett."

"Answer it." There's something in his tone that makes me think he's accustomed to giving orders and having them obeyed. It's at odds with everything I know about him, but I don't have time to think about it.

"Garrett?"

"We're done here. How…? Do I need to send that text?"

I look at Ronan. He's seemingly perfectly composed, but there's no sign of that tentative smile from earlier, and I find myself regretting the loss.

"Can we come up there yet? Ronan would like to speak with you before he begins work."

CHAPTER ELEVEN

Ronan

FOR THE FIRST TIME, I'm glad of the teleport sickness that overtakes me as we arrive in the cave. It gives me a precious few extra moments to process everything I've heard this morning. A few moments when Zac isn't waiting for a response from me.

Also for the first time, instead of stepping away and giving me time for the sickness to pass, today he hovers beside me. Not touching, not offering comfort, just *there*. I don't know if it's because of our truce or his guilt over what his grandmother did, but it's… nice.

The sickness slowly releases me from its clutches, and I straighten. Even though it always feels as though it's taking an eternity, I've noticed that I'm recovering more quickly now than I did the first few times. Maybe, eventually, I'll barely feel the effects at all.

That day can't come soon enough.

"Ronan?"

I turn toward the familiar voice. Garrett and Asher are coming toward me, Garrett's face openly reflecting his feelings. Asher's is harder to read, of course, but even I can see the traces of guilt and distress there—the same guilt and distress Zac has worn since his arrival at my house.

"Ronan, I am so sorry," Garrett begins.

"Thank you." I'm not sure what else to say. All my joy from last night feels so far away now. "Zac assured me that all the devices have been removed?"

He nods immediately and gestures to a bag Asher's holding. "We have them here. If you like, I can give you the schematic and software that was used to set up and monitor them, and you can compare the numbers. I also have the recorded results of the electronics sweep we just did, and of course, if you'd like to do one of your own, that's fine. I can't apologize enough for this."

"Another sweep isn't necessary, but I would appreciate if all the other records and information were sent to me." I don't feel the need to mention that as we speak, my magic is sweeping every inch of the cave for electronics. This isn't something I'm particularly good at, and due to my clumsiness, any other dragon would have immediately sensed what I was doing, but I'm good enough to know that they're not lying to me when they say all the devices have been removed. I give silent thanks to Steffen and his paranoid insistence on teaching me to do this last year.

"Zac has already agreed, but I would like your personal assurance that Damaris won't have access to the cave again while I'm working here."

Garrett shakes his head. "She won't. Nobody will who hasn't been personally vetted by me or the project security team, and anybody who comes here will be closely supervised the entire time."

I take a breath, my chest loosening a little. I believed Zac when he said it, but hearing Garrett reinforce it so vehemently helps. "Then, as I told Zac, I see no reason why a report should be made. There was a problem.

You've corrected it. My understanding of the situation is that reporting it now would just create the kind of instability our governments have worked hard to avoid." I close my mouth abruptly. There are some things I'm privy to, because of what *he* did, that I've been advised are classified at the highest level. I don't know how much these men know, and I'm not about to say more than I should. "Let's leave things there."

"Thank you." Asher speaks for the first time, and the intensity in his voice is almost hard to hear. "I'd like to add my personal apology to Garrett's and Zac's, and also apologize on behalf of our family. Grandmother will leave you be, Ronan. I swear it. If we have to, we'll take whatever steps are necessary to ensure it."

I don't know how to respond to that, so I only nod.

"We'll let you get to work," Garrett says, breaking the heavy tension. "Ah… I completely understand if all this has caused a change of heart, but if you're still interested, I'd love to come to movie night on Friday. I'd like us to be friends."

Hope, which was slowly smothered during Zac's revelation, sparks a tiny flame inside me. Maybe he's just trying to get on my good side after all this drama—Steffen would definitely say so—but Zoe was confident yesterday that Garrett would want to be my friend. I'm not my brother, and I'm willing to take this leap of faith.

I smile. "Me too. Movie night sounds good."

His relieved grin is balm to my soul. "How do you feel about karaoke?"

"No!" Asher and Zac shout in unison, and Garrett rolls his eyes.

"We'll talk about it Friday," he assures me. "I've gotta go get rid of all this crap. I'll send those data files to you this morning."

I nod, and Asher puts a hand on his husband's shoulder. They teleport out.

Zac heaves a giant sigh. "Do you want some coffee?" he asks abruptly, and I whip my head around to look at him. Offering each other drinks isn't something we do.

He shrugs, reading my expression correctly. "We're starting over, right? And you just stepped up and did us a huge service. The least I can do is make you a hot drink." A tiny grimace. "Plus I really need one right now."

I hear that loud and clear. "Tea, please. There should be some in that container." I point. "I'm going to open the vault, if you don't mind?"

He waves me off, already turning toward the designated "break" area. "Of course."

As I always do upon arrival, I assemble the vault handle the way Cam showed me and pull the door open. I need to use a tiny bit of magic to assist because it's so heavy. I have more muscle than Cam, but not quite as much as the demons I'm surrounded by.

Garrett and Asher have already turned on all the lights in the cave, including the ones near the vault entrance that light the first few yards inside. There are other, more portable lights waiting inside the vault for me to move around and arrange as I need them, but as I told Zac on Saturday, until I'm sure of which items can bear electric light exposure, I'm not taking any risks. My magic has been very useful in that regard.

I do my usual morning walk up the left aisle to the back of the vault, returning via the right aisle to the front. I don't expect anything to have moved or be different from how I left it, but it makes me feel better to check. The preservation spells that were placed on everything when they were stored still hold strong, even so many years after the death of the dragon who laid them. It's testament to her strength and the passion she had for this task.

I wish I could be even a quarter of the dragon she must have been.

"Ronan?"

I turn from staring blindly at the table where her message is burned into the surface. Zac is standing right outside the doorway to the vault, a steaming camping cup in each hand. He's been an absolute stickler for abiding by the security protocols put in place, never placing so much as a single foot inside the vault except for the time I needed help with a heavy item and asked him to come inside. That, more than anything, convinced me that he didn't know about the surveillance devices.

I join him outside the vault—I never bring food or drink inside—and take the cup he offers me. "Thank you." We stand there, sipping and mostly avoiding each other's gazes.

This is weird.

It's clear that we both want to make this truce work, but neither of us knows *how*. Zac would probably be better at it than me, but I'm sure he feels disadvantaged after this morning.

Luckily, as I drink my tea (the bag kind, but still good) and relax a little, I remember the tips my support group gave me last night.

I clear my throat. "How was babysitting yesterday?"

He gives me a startled look, then a hesitant smile. It's a demon smile, so I only see it because I'm paying very close attention. But it's still a smile, right?

"It was good. I took the kids—my little cousins, Chloe and Isaac—skating. The rink won't be there much longer, so they're eager to get as much time on it as they can." He hesitates for a second. "I know it might not feel like it to you, but spring is definitely on the way."

"I-I've noticed it's not always as snowy." I hadn't, really, but Zoe pointed it out yesterday, and I don't think she'll mind me borrowing her knowledge.

My phone dings in my pocket, but I ignore it.

"Yeah," Zac says. "Technically, it's already spring, but it looks different up here than it does elsewhere."

The conversation lags. That was a good start though, right? We actually spoke.

"So, uh," he says, "I heard you and Zoe went to the snow village yesterday."

My phone dings again, but I'm not letting it distract me. Zac's talking to me. "Yes, she came to introduce herself properly, and then when she found out dragons can self-regulate our body temperature, she decided I'm her new best friend."

He gives me a startled look, probably at the babble of oversharing. "Really? You can self-regulate body temp? I didn't know that."

Oh. I shrug. "Why would you? Unless you know a dragon personally, it's not something that comes up in trivia quizzes."

"So all this gear"—he gestures at my parka and hat—"you don't need it? Why do you wear it?"

I snort. "I'm trying to fit in."

His laugh is *amazing*. Not from an objective perspective—it's just an ordinary laugh—but *I* made it happen. He's laughing because of something I said. And not at me, in a mean way. I made a joke, and he laughed.

My phone dings again. And again.

He gestures toward my pocket. "Do you need to get that? It sounds like it might be important—your phone normally doesn't go off." His face flushes. "Not that I mean—"

"No, you're right," I say to forestall him thinking I'm offended by the implication that I have no friends. "I need to check it." Maybe something's happened to Steffen? But surely they'd call, not text.

I dig out the phone, look at the notifications on the screen, and groan.

"Is everything okay?" Zac's voice is concerned, and I flash him a smile.

"It's fine. It's… Do you remember Fabian? My friend who was here when I first arrived?"

He nods. "Sure. Chatty guy with dark hair."

"That's him. He's started this group chat and asked for suggestions on what to name it. And so far, they're all… terrible."

"Oh yeah? Like what?" He settles his feet slightly apart like he's prepared for a longer conversation.

I look back at the screen. "Well, there's 'Dragon Wagon' and 'Teething Problems.'"

He laughs again. "Teething Problems? What kind of group is this?"

Before I can answer, there's another ding.

"What's that one?" he asks.

Fuck. "Uh…" I can't think of anything made up. "Rescue Squad." It's actually "Ronan's Rescue Squad," but I'm not telling him that.

"Who are you all planning to rescue?"

I roll my eyes and try to laugh it off. "That was Hagen's suggestion. I don't know him all that well, but he's got a reputation for being weird. Let me mute this. They could be at it for a while." I tap out a quick message to say I'm working and will update them later, then turn the phone to silent mode and shove it back in my pocket.

Zac tips the cup to his lips, then says, "I'm going to get started on some stuff, but if you need anything, just yell out. Want me to let you know when it's time for lunch?"

I hope the way my breath catches isn't obvious. We don't normally eat lunch together—I'll come out of the vault when I'm hungry, and sometimes he's already eaten, sometimes he eats later. This is an olive branch.

"That would be great. Thanks."

CHAPTER TWELVE

Zac

"And if you go this way," I trace my finger along the map, "the terrain is a lot rougher, but when you get to this plateau…" Letting my words trail off, I spread my hands. "It's one of the more beautiful views I've ever seen."

This week has gone by in an odd combination of stilted conversations and completely relaxed chats. Sometimes it's so easy to talk to him, and I feel like we're becoming friends… or at least *could*. I really like those moments when Ronan is relaxed, his handsome face open. Other times, it just feels awkward, like we're trying too hard.

But at least we *are* trying. Even when we're both working on our separate jobs and the cave is quiet, the silence is friendlier. And it's nice to have someone to talk with over lunch—I really only like solitude when I'm out in nature and the planet and animals are there to keep me company.

Today, between bites of his sandwich, Ronan casually mentioned that he's curious about the area. "I've never lived at this altitude before," he said. "And I rarely visit anywhere mountainous—mostly I stick to where dragons have settled. What are some good places to explore?"

It's one of my favorite subjects, and I pulled out a map so fast, he actually startled. But he was quick enough to lean in and listen intently to what I said.

"What's the altitude like in this area?" he asks, using his finger to circle the trail I just pointed out. "Oh—what's a safe altitude for you Earth species?"

That's a weird question. "All the trails I've shown you are at a hike-able altitude for a physically fit adult, though I recommend taking it in easy stages and drinking a lot of water. But none of these trails are open right now. You need to wait until summer—late June at least. Some years, they wouldn't be safe until July. If you want to hike while there's still snow on the ground, there's some trails closer to the village. Even in winter, it's stunning around here. But you can't go alone—not unless I've cleared you to do so. It's a village by-law." It's just not safe for people to go wandering around in the snowy mountains willy-nilly. The council introduced the by-law forty-five years ago, after the third time we almost lost someone to frostbite and exposure. And those were adult demons capable of teleporting home. Now, if anybody wants to go hiking in winter, they have to have a permit issued by me. I don't issue permits to anyone who's not properly equipped, and I never issue permits to lone hikers unless I'm convinced of their survival skills.

"Oh, I wasn't thinking of hiking," he says absently, still studying the map. "This plateau... how big is it, exactly?"

I don't answer. I'm too busy trying to work out why he's asking if he doesn't want to hike it.

He lifts his head to look at me. "What are the conditions like around the plateau right now? Are they the same as outside this cave?"

My jaw drops as my brain fits the puzzle together. "You want to *fly* up there?"

He nods, his brown eyes earnest. "I thought Zoe might like to see it while it's still all snowy. She's been really kind to me. But I don't want to say anything to her and then find out it's not a safe altitude."

I. Am. Such. A. Jackass.

If I had gone out of my way to be nice to Ronan—or at least not actively been a prick to him—would he have found it easier to settle in here? Would this side of him, this part that clearly gives a shit about people and wants to *do nice things for them*, have shown itself sooner?

"I don't know enough about what conditions you can fly in," I manage. "Uh… the plateau is at a slightly lower elevation than this cave, though when you hike up, it doesn't feel like it because you have to get over this ridge first." I gesture to the ridge in question. "So it should be a lot calmer—less blowing snow and ice. There, uh…" I try to remember what all the rescue chopper pilots have told me. "There's usually a pretty strong eddy around here, though. I'm not sure how bad it gets in the winter." What else will he need to know? "Uh—it'll be cold up there. Really cold. I know that's not a problem for you, but Zoe would be exposed to—"

"I can keep her warm," he interrupts. "There's a spell for that. And I'll go up for a flight on my own first to make sure I can handle the conditions before I try to take her."

I chew my lip and try not to be envious. That view is one of my favorites, ever, of everything I've seen in the world—and I've traveled a lot. I can't teleport up to the plateau in winter to see it because there's no way to know what the snowdrifts look like—no definite landmark to go to. For that alone, I'd be envious. But to be able to see it from the back of a dragon?

"And… you can make sure she wouldn't fall? The conditions might be okay for you to fly in, but would she be able to stay on your back?"

He nods, studying the map again. "Yes, I have a harness that will hold her in place. But I would never let her fall, no matter what." He frowns. "I might need help with the harness. We didn't think of that."

Before I can ask who "we" is, he pulls out his phone and begins typing. I go back to studying the map. As a demon with teleportation ability, there aren't many places in these mountains I haven't been to. All I need is a visual identifier, and I can go there. Aerial surveillance photos, especially from satellites, can work just fine… as long as there's somewhere for me to *stand* in those images. There's no point teleporting to a stunning half-mile-high waterfall when the foliage around the bottom is so thick, I can't see where to go. Crashing thirty feet through a canopy of trees is a good way to get injured. Let's not even talk about the dangers of landing in the water itself.

I'm licensed to fly a helicopter, but it's hard to feel part of the natural beauty around you with the roar of the rotors and the artificial wind they cause disrupting the air. Not to mention, during the winter, flying a helicopter can be tricky in these mountains. Even if the wind conditions are good for flying, being in the wrong place at the wrong time can set off some pretty frightening avalanches.

A dragon, though… a dragon would be part of it all.

Ronan's phone dings. "Okay, my friends are going to put together detailed instructions and a diagram of how to put the harness on. Then Zoe can do it—I'm sure she can convince someone to help her." He smiles at me. "Thank you. I've been trying to think of a way to show her how much I appreciate her friendship."

"You're welcome. I can help—with the harness," I find

myself offering. "When the time comes. Just let me know." I grope for something else to say, a distraction from the pleasure that lights his face. "Uh, I'd want to be sure Zoe's properly kitted out anyway. You know, with a satellite phone… and water. Just in case something happens to you. Which I'm sure it won't," I rush to add. "But it's my job. To make sure everyone is safe out there." I wave my hand vaguely around, encompassing the cave, the alps, and the whole damn world. Who knows? I sure as fuck don't.

Ronan's nodding solemnly, though. "Of course. I would hate for Zoe to be stranded and unprepared if something did go wrong. Do satellite phones have cameras? In case she needs to send you a location photo. I can buy her a camera." He frowns. "But the photo would need to get from the camera to the phone… I wonder if I can get one with Bluetooth."

I need to change the subject before I start hating myself even more. "I've got everything she might need and can lend it to you. So what's this I hear about movie night tonight?"

His smile returns. I rarely ever saw it before this week —not this genuine version—and now it seems to be popping out every time I turn around. It's a great smile, too—warm and with something around the edges that makes me think that if he let his walls all the way down, he might be just a bit mischievous.

I'd like to meet *that* Ronan.

"Zoe planned it. She says it's a good excuse to stuff ourselves with junk food—and then she conned me into making pastries." He rolls his eyes, but his pleased expression tells me he doesn't really mind.

"You bake?" Belatedly, I remember the streak of flour he was wearing last weekend, and I backpedal fast, not wanting to kill his happy vibes. "That's great. Zoe loves good food, so if she's conning you into baking, she must think you're a master baker." I hide my wince at the accidental dirty pun, but he doesn't seem to get it.

Instead he laughs. "I'm not even close. I'm not even a baker, really. Kethe let me help her a few times when—uh, when I was staying at Here Be Dragons." There's a sudden tension in his voice, and I don't know what put it there. "And then last week I needed to fill some time, so I watched some YouTube videos and made croissants. Zoe decided that qualifies me to make treats for tonight."

He watched some YouTube videos and made croissants that Zoe thought were good enough that she needed him to bake something else? Either Zoe feels *really* sorry for him and wants to boost his confidence, or he's a hell of an intuitive baker.

"Sounds qualified enough for me," I say. "I'm a terrible baker. I make a mean soup, though." That's not bragging. Anytime I get the urge to drag out the big soup pot, my cousins cancel their plans.

"Soup's good," Ronan says. "It warms you from the inside." He flushes. "That sounds stupid. All hot food does that. I just mean, there's something about soup..." He trails off, looking embarrassed.

"No, I get it. Soup is one of those foods that feeds your body and your soul." It's my turn to feel embarrassed. I've never said that out loud before—my cousins, even though they love my soups, would laugh themselves into comas.

But Ronan sighs in relief. "Yes. That's it exactly. It makes everything feel okay." He shrugs. "Maybe that's because it's not that quick to make. I can grill a steak and vegetables in less than half an hour from the decision to sitting down to eat. But with soup... it takes time. Someone has to take the time."

Unspoken is the implication that someone has to care

enough to take the time, and I wonder what happened to make that so important to him. The way he is, sometimes, it's like he doesn't know how to be comfortable around people. But everything I've heard about dragons has pointed to them being very close-knit and protective of each other.

Maybe it's something he and his brother went through? Fuck knows, Steffen Draco is weird. He scares the crap out of me, and I don't scare easy. Plus, Gideon made sure to tell us all *not* to piss him off or do anything that might be perceived as threatening. When Asher asked why, he just shook his head and said, "I'd rather not have to start an interspecies war on your behalf."

So maybe it was just growing up with Steffen for a twin that's made Ronan unsure of how to deal with people. Or it could be the fact that, I don't know, he lost his homeland and whole world and now has to get used to a new one? It hasn't been *that* many years, especially when you consider how long-lived dragons are. At least when I miss my old home, I can go back and visit.

The dragons can never go home.

CHAPTER THIRTEEN

Ronan

"Wait, so... the planet they crashed on is *Earth* in the past?" Cam shoves a handful of popcorn into his mouth as a huge lizard-looking creature—though I've never seen a lizard that size—attacks the valiant hero.

"This movie is so fucked-up," Garrett moans, but his fascinated gaze is fixed on the screen. "Are we really supposed to believe that life on a distant planet evolved to create humans over sixty-five million years ago, and then the process was repeated here exactly the same way? Be real. The least they could have done was made them look different or given them a nonhuman ability like telekinesis."

I look from the screen to them, then back at the screen. Something has clearly told them that this primitive planet is Earth, but I don't get it.

Leaning closer to Zoe, I murmur, "How do we know this is Earth?"

I should have remembered that Garrett's hellhound ears are far more sensitive than those of any other species, because the question is barely out of my mouth before he's snatching up the remote control and hitting Pause.

"What?" Cam asks. "It was starting to get good. The dinosaur might have won!"

"It's not that kind of movie," Zoe tells him kindly. "I'm pretty sure the good guy's going to win."

Cam pulls a face. "I'm less interested now. Does the girl die, at least?"

"I haven't seen it, so I don't know. But the reason Garrett paused is because Ronan's never seen a dinosaur before."

All eyes turn to me, and I resist the urge to squirm. "Earth has a lot of history," I defend weakly. "I-I'm still working through it all. I wanted to learn about all the different modern cultures first." Which, as they've all probably guessed, hasn't exactly been a strong point. Partly because I've been focused on trying to learn about my own culture—and it goes back a lot more than sixty-five million years.

"No, no, that's cool. It's just… Does that mean you've never seen *Jurassic Park*?" Cam's eyes are wide.

I bite my lip. We've all been having a good time so far, and I don't want to wreck it. "No, I haven't. Is… is it in America?"

"We must stop this movie immediately," Garrett declares. "Where's *Jurassic Park* streaming?"

While Zoe and Cam bend their heads to their phones, Garrett smiles at me. "The dinosaurs predated our modern species here on Earth by about 250 million years. Then sixty-five million years ago, an asteroid hit the planet, setting off a chain reaction that led to an ice age and the eventual extinction of most of them."

"Most of them? There are still some alive?" I look at the frozen image on the screen. I'm pretty sure I would have heard about it if something like that was still roaming the planet.

"Not exactly. I'm not all that knowledgeable in this field, but I believe some of the avian species evolved into our modern-day birds. And crocodiles and alligators are also descended from dinosaurs."

That's really interesting. "So did they really look like that?" I gesture at the screen.

Garrett shrugs. "We're not completely sure what they looked like," he replies, still using his teaching tone. "Or what they sounded like. I think some of the more recent theories posit that instead of lizard hides, some of them were feathered. Our information all comes from fossils and guesswork."

"And they've been dead for sixty-five million years?" I guess Earth has some pretty cool history too.

"Give or take. That's when the asteroid hit the planet."

Cam looks up. "Hey, if the movie's called *65*, does that mean the asteroid is going to hit while they're there?" His eyes widen. "Because that would be a cool ending. Like, they go through all this crap, fighting off dinosaurs, and then at the end, kaboom."

"I still don't think it's that kind of movie," Zoe says patiently. "Does Micah know you're this bloodthirsty?"

"Oh yeah. We had a *Scream* marathon a few weeks back. At first he was shocked, but then I think it kind of turned him on. When we had sex that night, he did the th—"

Garrett clamps a hand over Cam's mouth. "No. He's practically Asher's brother, which means he's like my brother. I'm happy you have a satisfying sex life together, and if you ever run into problems, I'll be there to troubleshoot, but no. There will be no details that might make it hard for me to look him in the eye tomorrow."

Cam rolls his eyes but nods, and Garrett removes his hand. "Fine. No details. Prude. *Jurassic Park* is streaming on Netflix and Prime."

Zoe looks over at me. "Do you mind if we change movies? We can always come back to this one later, but believe me, *Jurassic Park* is better."

"My dinosaur education is in your hands." This is fun! Who knew friendship could be so easy?

Cam cheers. "We need more snacks! And a pee break. Meet back here in five."

ᘻ

"THE THING IS," Cam says, hours later, after both movies have been watched and many of my questions answered, "if the asteroid hadn't hit, there's a really good chance none of our species would have evolved. Right, Garrett?" He's lying on the floor, staring up at the ceiling, eyes narrowed.

"There's no way to know for sure," Garrett replies. He's curled up in a corner of Zoe's couch, eating what's left of the popcorn. I thought we dragons ate a lot, but so far, Garrett's matched me bite for bite… and then some.

"Sure, but I'm probably right. So… the humans shouldn't be making up all these fake gods. They should be worshiping the asteroid."

We all stop to think about that one.

"It might be a hard sell," Zoe says finally. "They like to pretend their gods can talk to them. A big hunk of space rock can't do that."

Cam blows a raspberry. "Humans are weird."

"That's the truth," Zoe agrees. "How would it have been for dragons, Ronan? If you'd started visiting here and the planet was populated by dinosaurs?"

Cam sits up suddenly. "*Did* dragons and elves visit here when the planet was populated by dinosaurs?"

Garrett inhales so sharply, he chokes on a popcorn kernel. "Please," he wheezes, "please! The history… please!"

I shake my head. "Sorry. I don't know exactly when the elves opened the first portal to here, but the modern species had already evolved. They discovered a few other planets that were compatible with our bodies' needs, but none of them had species with higher intelligence, so nobody bothered with them again."

Garrett subsides, his eyes still watering. "It was too good to be true," he rasps. Zoe hands him his drink, and I take a second to be grateful they asked something I actually know the answer to. The version of history I was taught growing up differed a lot from reality, and I still find myself learning things that aren't what I thought they were.

Yawning, Cam lies back down. "Zoe, can I sleep here tonight? I don't even need a bed. This floor is fine."

Zoe shrugs. "Sure. But you know, one of the benefits of dating a demon is that if you call him, he'll come and teleport you home. Knowing Micah, you wouldn't even need to stand. He'd just scoop you up and bam—next thing, you'd be in your bed."

Cam flips a hand. "True, but I'm teaching him a lesson."

"Oooh," Garrett and Zoe say together, and I find myself leaning forward.

"This, I want you to tell me," Garrett insists. "What did he do?"

"We were talking about Zac's ski resort." Cam pauses. "Well, *I* was talking about Zac's ski resort. I just don't get why suddenly it's been shelved and nobody wants to discuss it. It's a great idea, right? And I was trying to get Micah to agree to talk to Zac about it, and he went all stone-faced and said," he lowers his voice in mockery of his boyfriend, "Leave it alone, Cam. It's not up for discussion."

Zoe gasps. "He did *not*."

I purse my lips. "Um." Should I say anything? I'm afraid to ruin things, but if he was comfortable discussing it in front of me, he probably won't mind. And friends give opinions, right? "I don't know much about your relationship, but that doesn't seem like the way Micah talks to you?"

"It's not," they all three say in unison.

"Micah *adores* Cam," Zoe adds. "It's almost sickening, sometimes. I've never heard about him saying no to something Cam wants, especially something so harmless." She pauses. "What ski resort, though? This is the first I've heard of it, and I love to ski. I mean, snow, yeah?"

"It was an idea Zac had," Garrett says slowly. His brow is furrowed. "What, a few weeks ago? A month? I think I heard about it around the time Ronan arrived."

Cam nods. "Yep. He was looking at papers and working some plans out when Micah and I went to get him to teleport everyone to the cave."

"It was a good idea." Garrett still seems thoughtful. "It needed more research, but... You know, now I think of it, Asher shut me down the last time I mentioned it to him. And last week at dinner, when you brought it up, Zac got all weird."

"What did he say?" I ask, my heartbeat picking up slightly. Maybe this ski resort is another way I can connect with Zac. Things between us this week have been... okay. Almost good. Today was good. Maybe if I show him I can support his project, he and I can start to be friends. Not that I know anything about skiing. But I can learn, right? I didn't know anything about dragons, either, until five years ago.

"He said it would be good for the village, and it sounded like he's still invested, but he also said it's shelved."

"And then Damaris had her tantrum," Cam adds, rolling his eyes again, "and the subject got changed."

From the corner of my eye, I notice Garrett stiffening slightly, and I realize with a little shock that Damaris's tantrum was probably about me. The whole incident with the surveillance devices and what Zac said to me.

"Damaris had a tantrum?" Zoe shudders. "Please don't ever invite me to Sunday dinner, then. I get freaked out by her when she's in a good mood."

"It does seem odd that Zac would still want the resort but nobody's willing to talk about it," I interrupt, partly to steer the conversation away from Damaris's tantrum and partly because I'm now extremely intrigued by this ski resort. "Could there maybe have been a problem with the plans themselves?"

Cam rolls onto his side and props his head on his hand. "I didn't see very much of them," he admits, "and I wouldn't know how to recognize a problem if I did, unless it was something mechanical."

"I didn't see the plans at all, just heard them spoken about," Garrett adds.

Zoe sighs. "I guess we'll never know. Not unless it all gets unshelved."

Deep inside me, in that place I've been stifling my whole life, an idea sparks. It's stupid and reckless, and the intelligent side of my brain pushes it away. *I don't do things like that.*

Don't you? The tool raised by him *never would. But what about the dragon you?*

"Or we can look at the plans and see for ourselves." The words are out of my mouth before I can second-guess them, the spark of an idea taking full shape. "If there really is a problem, then fine. But if there isn't..." My neck starts to get hot. The three of them are staring at me. Zoe's jaw is dropped. Cam's blinking fast.

Garrett, though... Garrett's grinning.

That grin gives me the courage to continue. "If there isn't a problem with the plans themselves, then maybe all the resort needs is some champions. And... and we might not be on the village council, but Garrett's in charge of an intergovernmental project that's going to make a big impact here, and Zoe is a huge part of the plan to attract other species here. And Cam opened the vault door—he's a hero right now. And I... uh, I know a lot of dragons." That's true.

"Okay," Zoe says. "But if nobody wants to talk about the resort, they're not likely to hand over the plans for us to see."

"So we steal them." Did I say that? Oh blessed ether, did I say that? "Where would they be?" It's like my mouth is working independently from my brain. Is this what it's like to be a real dragon?

I take in the way my companions' faces are alight with excitement. Is this what it's like to be fun?

"In the house. Probably in Zac's room." Garrett shrugs. "That's easy enough—I can look on Monday when everyone else is at work and he takes you to the cave."

"Monday?" Zoe whines, even as Cam says, "I can't wait that long."

"Can you keep it secret from Asher and Micah that long?" I ask. My only experience of people in relationships is what I've seen from my dragon friends, and I know for sure that Fabian and Dustin tell their boyfriends everything.

Sure enough, Cam and Garrett exchange a glance. "I mean," Cam says, sitting up and somehow bumping his elbow on the coffee table, "I maybe could if I stayed here all weekend."

Garrett shakes his head. "That won't work. Micah will come over tomorrow to beg you to come home. If you say no, then you'll start a real fight."

"I don't think I could say no anyway," Cam concedes. "He's so adorable when he begs."

Micah? Adorable? Love must really mess with people's brains.

"So we do it tomorrow," Zoe suggests. This time it's Cam who shakes his head.

"It's Saturday. They'll all be home, and it'll be harder for one of us to search Zac's room."

"It has to be tonight." My mind is whirling. "What time is it?" We all turn to look at the clock on the wall. Just before midnight. Perfect. "Who's at the house now?"

"They were going to hang out tonight," Garrett says, "but Asher was up super early this morning, so I bet he's gone to bed already. He gets cranky when he hasn't had enough sleep."

"If Asher's gone to bed, Micah would be at home," Cam volunteers. "I was snotty before I left, so he's probably waiting for me to come back." He frowns. "He better apologize soon so I can forgive him."

"Okay, but even if Asher sleeps like the dead, *Zac's* still there. I don't think we can search his room if he's in it. We need to get him out of the house."

Damn. We fall silent. How do we get him out of the house at midnight? It's not like there's a nightclub around here we can invite him to. We need a distraction.

"Zoe, tell me you're afraid of heights," I demand.

They all look at me like I've lost my sanity. "What?"

"Tell me you're afraid of heights."

"Uh… but I'm no—"

"Zoe!"

"Okay, sure. I'm afraid of heights. Terrified. Throw up at the sight of a stepladder."

I nod. "Be ready. I'm going home, and I'm going to call Zac and tell him I need his help. When he leaves, you three sneak in and find the plans."

They're back to staring at me.

"Yeah, sorry, we're going to need more than that," Zoe says eventually. "For starters, I know you and Zac are getting along better now, but I didn't think you were besties or anything."

For a second, I debate whether to keep it a secret still. But fuck it—this plan is more important. "Surprise," I tell her. "I was planning to take you up for a flight in my dragon form. To see the snowy Alps from the air."

She gasps, then throws herself into my arms. "Oh, *Ronan*! That's the most amaz— I mean, oh no, I'm scared of heights!" She kisses my cheek. "But if I wasn't, I'd be telling you that's the best surprise anyone ever gave me."

My face is hot. "You've been nice to me," I mumble. "I wanted to do something nice for you."

"Wait, but why is she scared of heights?" Garrett asks, and I pull my focus back to the task at hand.

"Today, I told Zac what I was planning, and he showed me some places on a map that I can take Zoe. If I call him and sound all panicky about needing to know where I can go if I have to stay within, say, twenty feet of the ground, he'll…" I trail off. Zac's not going to leave his house at midnight to come and look at a map for someone he barely knows. I sigh. "It won't work."

"Fuck if it won't," Cam says. "The Bailey cousins have a massive white knight complex. If you sound upset and apologize and say how all your plans are ruined and you can't sleep, he'll come to rescue you."

"It's like a compulsion," Garrett adds. "They can't help it. Just make him think it's a disaster. Do you think you could cry a little?"

This might be getting out of control. "I can use magic to make it seem like I'm crying?"

They both nod approvingly.

"Good enough." Garrett turns to Cam and Zoe. "Once Zac's gone, it'll be easy. Asher sleeps like the dead."

Cam instantly shakes his head. "Nope. I know my limitations. Sneaking around is not my forte. If I knock something over and break it, he'll know we've been there. I'll wait in the kitchen. That way, if Asher does wake up or Zac comes home early, I can distract them."

"And there's no reason for me to be in the house at all," Zoe says. "You being in Zac's room can be fobbed off. If I'm there, it looks suspicious. I'll wait outside and be look-out. But," she adds, "I've got this handy little weave that deadens sound. That way Asher definitely won't wake up."

I look around the group. "Are we all set? I'll go home and call Zac. You get ready to move. And then, as soon as you have the plans and you're outside again, text me so I can let him go home. Then we meet back here to look at the plans." I don't know how I'll keep him at my house if he solves the "problem" quickly and Garrett still hasn't found anything. But that's something for future me to worry about.

Wow, I'm really not myself tonight. I kinda like it. Fabian and the others won't believe this.

Zoe puts out her hand, palm down, and I stare at it. What…?

Cam and Garrett stack theirs on top, and then they all look at me expectantly. Hesitantly, I add mine to the pile.

"Goooooo, team!" they yell, throwing their hands up.

"Go, team." I'm a beat behind, but it counts.

I'm still part of the team.

CHAPTER FOURTEEN

Zac

THE STRIDENT RING of my phone drags me from sleep. What the fuck? I didn't get into bed until after eleven—who would call me at this time?

I grope for the device and hold it in front of my face. *Ronan Calling…* That wakes me all the way up. Why would Ronan be calling me this late? He's supposed to be at movie night—has something happened?

But if it had, why would he call me and not Asher or Micah?

I answer tensely. "Hello? Ronan?"

A noise that sounds suspiciously like a sob comes down the line, and I throw back the covers, reaching for my pants.

"Zac?" His voice quavers.

"What's wrong? Are you hurt?" I sandwich the phone between my shoulder and ear so I can zip up. "Are you still at Zoe's? Is everyone okay?"

"I'm home," he says. "But… but… I don't know what to do."

"Are you hurt?" I look around for a shirt. "Do you need a healer?"

"No. No, I'm… fine. It's stupid." The last is a whisper, and I sit down on the side of the bed with a wisp of relief. Is he drunk dialing me?

"I'm sure it's not stupid," I assure him, trying to sound soothing. "Ronan, have you been drinking? Did you have alcohol at Zoe's?"

"No. Just soda. Because Zoe said we'd have more fun if we could remember everything tomorrow. But now I just want to forget it all because she's not going to be my friend!" He makes another choked-tears sound, and I resist the urge to groan. Who knows what the fuck is going on, but it doesn't seem like getting the full story out of him is going to be easy.

"How about I come over and you can tell me all about it?" The words are out of my mouth before I can resist the impulse. I'm awake now, I'm mostly dressed, he's upset, and I said I was going to try to be his friend. It'll take me two seconds to teleport there, maybe fifteen minutes to calm him down, and I can be sleeping in my bed again within less than half an hour.

He hiccups, and sympathy slashes at my heart. Poor guy. He's been so happy about Zoe being his friend. I'm sure whatever the problem is, it can easily be cleared up.

"Could you?" He sounds so pathetic that even if I hadn't already decided, that would have done it.

"Of course. I'll be there in two minutes… just wait outside the teleport room."

"O-Okay." The call drops out, and I toss my phone aside while I put on my shirt and shoes. Then I teleport to his house.

When I open the door to the hall, he's hovering there,

wringing his hands, eyes looking a little red. His face crumples at the sight of me. "I don't know what to dooooo!"

"It's going to be okay," I promise, fervently hoping I can deliver on that. Slinging an arm around his shoulders, I steer him toward the living room. The light's on, and a map of the area is spread on the coffee table, surrounded by a few crumpled tissues. Together, we sit on the couch, and I say, "Now, tell me what happened. Did someone say something tonight?" I can't imagine that Zoe, Cam, or Garrett would say anything to turn him into this mess, but… didn't he mention something about Zoe not wanting to be his friend?

He sniffles. "We watched some movies and—did you know that you might not exist if the asteroid hadn't killed the dinosaurs?"

Um. What? I replay the sentence through my head. "I… guess so? I never really thought about it. Are you sure you were just drinking soda?" I'm positive that nobody would have spiked his drinks, but… "Did you maybe smoke something?"

He shakes his head. "We watched *Jurassic Park* and *65*, and we were talking about the asteroid, and Cam said that if it weren't for that, none of the Earth species might have existed."

"Sure." I go with it. "That seems likely. Is that what upset you? The thought that your new friends might not have existed?" Seems kind of sensitive, but some people are like that. And I can soothe that just by pointing out that they *do* exist.

"No. It's just interesting. Cam thinks *65* would have been more interesting if they'd died."

I haven't seen *65*, but I'm getting the feeling I'll hate it simply because it's associated with this conversation. "If who died? The dinosaurs? They did, eventually."

He rolls his eyes. "No, the humans. Though Garrett says we really shouldn't call them humans because it's unlikely a species from a distant planet so long ago evolved exactly the same way humans on this planet did. He thinks it's lazy scriptwriting."

I am definitely never going to watch this movie. I might also have to maim Garrett and Cam for all the weird commentary. Why is it taking Ronan so long to get to the point?

"That's a valid concern," I agree. "So… what upset you?"

His lip trembles. "Zoe's been so nice to me. She's helped me so much this week."

I nod encouragingly, patting his back.

"And tonight was so fun. I feel like I might be able to have friends here."

"You do have friends here." I try not to wince. It was an automatic response, and I'm not sure how true it is. Sure, Zoe befriended him, but there's some sort of issue with that. "Cam and Garrett like you a lot," I prevaricate. They were both eager for this movie night, anyway. "And we're getting along, right? I wouldn't have come over in the middle of the night for just anyone."

For a second, something that looks like guilt flashes across his face, but it's gone so fast, I must be mistaken.

"So, come on. Tell me what happened to upset you like this."

"Well… we were all talking… and… let me show you something." He jumps up and runs from the room, leaving me sitting on the couch like a lump and wondering what in the living fuck is actually going on right now.

Ronan staggers back into the room carrying a huge box, and I scramble up to help him. We set it on the floor beside the coffee table.

"What is this?"

He flips open the four flaps, revealing a large piece of paper with a diagram and written instructions, and what looks like a pile of leather straps underneath.

"It's the harness," he says dolefully. "The one I was going to use to take Zoe flying."

I shove aside the pang of jealousy and nod. "Yeah. You told me about it. I can still help her get it on you if you want."

"But… but…"

I wait.

"Zoe's scared of heights!"

I wait a bit more as he buries his face in his hands, his shoulders shaking. Is… that it? "Are you sure?" I'm pretty sure I've seen her up on ladders. And we talked one time about this hike that hugs the wall of a ravine—she didn't seem put off by the idea.

He nods and says something that's muffled by his hands. I had no idea he could be so dramatic. This fits a bit more with the stuff I'd heard about dragons. Maybe Ronan's like Garrett—reserved and mature, but deep down, still sharing the same traits as the rest of his species.

Gently clasping his wrists, I tug his hands down. "Say that again."

He looks up at me with wide, sad eyes. "She said she was. I didn't even get a chance to ask her if she wanted to." He looks down and sniffles again. "And now she'll see I can't even be an equal friend and she'll get sick of me."

This is not really happening to me. If it was Cam or Garrett doing this, I'd be looking around for Asher and Micah and asking who masterminded the prank. But Ronan's face is so earnest…

"Maybe she's just scared of big heights," I attempt. "I've seen her on ladders. Can you, I don't know, fly low?

That way she'll feel like there isn't as far to fall. Not that you'd let her fall," I add hastily, gesturing to the box full of harness. "I'm sure even without this seat belt thing, you'd catch her."

He nods fervently. "I would." A shaky breath. "Do you think that might work? Flying low?"

"You could ask her. And that would get her even closer to the snow, so she'll love that."

Chewing on his lip, he thinks about it. "Maybe. But flying low can be so dangerous. I'd need to make sure I have enough clearance space, and then there's wind shear off the mountain…" He looks at me hopefully. "Do you think… Can you tell me about some of the conditions along the way to the plateau? Closer in to the trail than I was expecting to fly, I mean."

I look over at the map spread on the coffee table, then at my Smartwatch. "I can, but… maybe you should get some rest. Things will look brighter in the morning, and we can plan your whole route then."

He shakes his head vehemently. "No! I mean… I don't think I'll be able to sleep until this is settled. I'll just keep worrying that it might not be possible. And I really, really want to show Zoe how glad I am she's my friend." He puts a hand on my arm. "Please, Zac. I know it's a lot to ask, but I promise, I'll pay you back. I'll do everything I can to make sure your dreams come true."

I'd probably think that's a weird thing for him to say, but it's the middle of the night after a long week, and he's feeling emotional. Plus… dragon drama. I get it now, why Gideon always mutters darkly about them. If I had to deal with a whole lot of dragons being this dramatic in my job, I'd be muttering too, and I'm not the one we used to call Murder Baby.

"Sure," I concede. "Let's take a look now." His face

lights up, and the last traces of distance I might have felt toward him melt away. How can I not like someone who wants so badly to do something nice for a friend?

For the next twenty minutes, we trace along the route he would have to take, with me scraping my memory for every detail I know and him making careful notes. There's a lot I'm not completely sure of—I can't get to some parts of the trail in winter, so I'm not sure how the snow accumulates, exactly, or where icicles might form that he'd need to steer clear off. The wind seems to be the part that concerns him the most—he can see other obstacles, but wind shear is unpredictable, and the last thing he needs is to be driven into the side of a mountain.

I'm just calculating whether it would be safer for him to skim the top of the ridge or fly alongside it most of the way when his phone chimes. He snatches it up so fast, his hands almost blur, but whatever he reads brings a relieved smile to his face.

"Everything okay?" I ask casually. "It's kind of late for a text."

"Friend from home. Time difference. But wow, you know, it really is late." He yawns. "I'm so sorry, Zac. I've dragged you here and kept you awake… I'll bet you're exhausted. And you were right; I feel so much better with the idea of flying low. By tomorrow morning, I'll be excited about it again." The words tumble out so fast, it takes my tired brain a second to make sense of them. By then, he's looped his arm in mine and dragged me up from the couch.

"I'm so grateful for your help, but we can finish this later. Please go home and get some rest." He smiles at me, the genuine one I've seen a few times this week.

"Are you sure?" I check. I don't want to look a gift

horse in the mouth, but I also don't want to find out later that he was awake and miserable all night.

"I'm sure. Thank you. You're a good man." He leans in and kisses my cheek. "I know we're still not there, but I hope we can be friends."

"Of course." It's an automatic reply. In fact, my whole body seems to be on autopilot as Ronan guides me toward the teleport room. I don't even think to tell him that I don't need to leave from there, just arrive. I'm home again and back in my bed before I can fully process what just happened.

Ronan kissed me. On the cheek, like a friend would.

And I wanted it to be more.

How fucked-up is that?

CHAPTER FIFTEEN

Ronan

I BURST into Zoe's house, panting from running the three blocks over. The night air is sharp and cold and made my lungs burn, but I couldn't handle any kind of delay. "Well?" I demand, slamming the front door and racing toward the living room. "Have you looked?"

My friends—because I think after tonight's adventure, I can call them that—have pushed the coffee table aside and spread an assortment of paper on the floor.

"We're looking," Cam reports. "Though honestly, I'm not even sure what some of this *is*."

I drop to my knees beside him and peer at the papers. There are a lot of them. "Are we sure he won't notice they're missing?"

"Pretty sure," Garrett says. "I took them out of the folders he was using and put blank paper in there instead. So unless he actually opens the folders to look before I can sneak everything back in on Monday, it should be fine." He squints at the document he's reading. "We might need longer than a few days. I'm going to start taking photos of everything. Do any of you know anything about site excavation and construction engineering?"

"No, but his business plan is pretty good." Zoe's tone is thoughtful as she turns a page. "He's got a lot of details here, and cost projections…" She trails off as she looks up to find us staring at her. "What? I have friends who run their own businesses. I even helped with some research once. Cam, you're a business owner—what do you think of this?"

We pore over the papers, putting aside the technical ones we're going to need help with and focusing on the rest. Zoe's right—the basic plan is a good one. From what information we can find on the internet, Zac's cost projections and financial forecasting are pretty solid too.

"So it comes down to two things, then," Garrett says finally, sitting back on his haunches. "Whether the land is fit for purpose, and whether people would even want to come here for skiing."

"Absolutely yes to the second," Zoe insists. "Trust me on this. A community-only ski resort with a long season, a quaint village, and a local site of historic interest? I could make a few calls to some friends in the winter sports arena and have the first season sold out within a month. You have no idea how many parents stress about letting their kids participate in sports in front of humans. The chances of something unusual being noticed are so much higher. Take that factor out of the equation, and this will become the family-friendly winter destination of choice."

"What about storms?" Garrett counters. "You were here through most of the winter—people aren't going to be happy about paying for skiing they can't do because they're trapped indoors."

"Day trips?" Cam suggests. "You were trying to find an elf who'd open regular portals, right? The museum and definitely the resort won't work if people can't get here. But maybe we expand that service—on days when skiing and other outdoor activities aren't possible, and people don't want to stay indoors, they can take a day trip to Zurich. Or anywhere—find an events coordinator who can put together packages."

"Hmm." I think about that. I'm used to portal travel, myself, having grown up with it—though I never really went anywhere—but for species who rely on slower means of transportation, the idea of being able to have a multi-destination vacation with such little fuss would probably be a bonus. "Have you found an elf who can help? Because the whole idea lives or dies on that."

Garrett nods. "Yeah, I think so. Alistair's friend Caolan put me in touch with an elf who retired from the royal guard a few years back. She's bored and seemed really interested in the idea. I could probably talk her into doing more than the twice-daily portals to Zurich we'd already discussed. Or she might know somebody else."

The number of elves who can open portals is very limited, and most of them are in service to the King or the DEA. It's not likely there will be many of them looking for a new job, but one might be enough—to start with, at least.

"So the only thing we're really not sure about is the land, then." Cam picks up the technical papers. "Could that be why Zac shelved it? He found out something that would make it impossible?"

We crowd around, trying to decipher things we know nothing about. "We need help," I finally decide.

Zoe sits back with a sigh. "Yeah, but who can we ask? Micah would be ideal, but then Cam would lose the high ground in their argument."

"Not happening," Cam insists. "I don't want to set that kind of precedent."

I chew my lip. "Let me ask my friends. They know a lot of people." If it comes right down to it, I can ask Steffen and Wil. They definitely have contacts who'd be able to help. But I'm pretty sure if I tell my paranoid conspiracy-theorist security-obsessed brother what I did tonight, he'll have some kind of seizure.

Fabian, on the other hand, will probably be proud.

"Can we trust them?" Garrett asks, and I shrug.

"It's not a security issue, so I think they'll keep it secret." I grab my phone and open the group chat... which still doesn't have a name, though the suggestions are getting more and more outlandish.

> I need some help! Does anyone know someone who can look at engineering and construction reports and tell if the land is fit for purpose?

I hope that makes sense. I'm not even sure if that's what these reports are called. They're just full of numbers and equations and words that make no sense to me.

I can see people typing immediately.

DUSTIN:

> Hiiiiiii! You're up late! Please tell me you're at a party and not working.

SOPHIE:

> Honey, why are you looking at boring reports? And what are you building?

FABIAN:

> Ummmm I fucked an engineer one time but I don't remember his name.

> This is all a secret… we broke into Zac's room and stole the plans for the ski resort he wants to build but then suddenly nobody will talk about. And now we can't read some of the stuff.

There's a moment of absolute nothing in the chat, and I bite my lip. Was that too much all at once?

FABIAN:

Who's we?

DUSTIN:

I am so PROUD of you!

SOPHIE:

I thought we were befriending Zac? Why are we stealing from him?

> We're going to put it back. Wait a sec

The explanation is too long to type, so while Zoe, Garrett, and Cam watch, I send a voice message with the short version of everything that happened tonight.

FABIAN:

Ohhhhhh. Okay, we can help! Not me, though. Where's Hagen?

DUSTIN:

Calling him now… could he still be at work?

HAGEN:

What is WRONG with you people? I was just about to get head from my hot vampire boyfriend, and my phone starts blowing up! Now he's all "it might be important" and won't touch me until I check it!

SOPHIE:

LISTEN TO RONAN'S MESSAGE

There's a short delay.

HAGEN:

> Oh yeah, I can help with that. After I get head, though. Send me the reports, and I'll have a look later.

I blink at the screen. He can help? *Hagen?* I don't want to question his expertise, but… most of what I've heard about him has been along the lines of "irresponsible fuckboy."

DUSTIN:

> Perfect! Hagen's a specialist in operations planning and rollout, Ronan. He knows enough about this stuff to say if the resort is feasible on that land.

I exhale with relief and send a silent thanks to Dustin.

> Thank you! I'll send them now. Enjoy your head.

Blinking, I wonder if I can take back that message. Did I really write…?

HAGEN:

> Oh, I will.

SOPHIE:

> So glad you're making friends! Keep being nice to Zac. If he finds out you robbed him, you'll need some goodwill stocked up.

> We didn't rob him. We're putting it all back!

FABIAN:

> Meh. Either way… you're making us all proud to know you.

DUSTIN:

But NOBODY tell Steffen about this.

There's a round of heartfelt agreements, and then the chat falls quiet. I look up at the expectant faces. "Good news. Hagen's apparently an expert in operational planning and rollout." Whatever that is. "He can look at the papers and tell us what they mean. We just have to send him copies."

"That's great!" Cam claps his hands. "Can he do it now?"

I'm not going to tell them what Hagen's actually doing right now. "Uh, we should send them now, but he might need time to go through them. So we can probably go to bed."

"Good plan," Garrett says firmly when it looks like Zoe and Cam might protest. "We're all going to need to be rested to deal with tomorrow. If we have to demand answers, we want to be at our best."

An image rises in my mind of the four of us facing down Zac, Asher, and Micah. Sure, they're big, intimidating demons, but we're not helpless. Garrett's a hellhound… academic. And Cam's an incubus… who trips over his feet walking in a straight line. Zoe's a sorcerer—she could throw some snow at them. I'm a dragon. My magic is pretty badass… but I want them to like me.

This might be a problem.

"Relax," Zoe tells me, almost like she's reading my mind. "It's gonna be fine. Cam and Garrett will use their wiles on Micah and Asher, and we can handle Zac. We're on his side. He'll get over being mad."

"I have wiles?" Cam wonders. "What are wiles?"

"You know when you smile at Micah and he melts into

a puddle of goo and does anything you ask for? Those are wiles," Garrett explains.

Cam nods. "Ohhhh. Yeah, I can do that. I always give him rewards after I wile him. They're fun for me too."

"My wiles aren't as good as Cam's, but I can manage Asher," Garrett assures me confidently. "And I really think he and Micah want this to happen for Zac, anyway. We just have to rush past the part where we stole and get to the bit where we're going to help… you know, if it's even feasible."

"If it's not, then we don't have anything to worry about. You're all staying here, right?" Zoe starts yanking cushions off the couch, revealing a fold-out sofa bed. "There's a bed in the spare room too. You're going to have to fight it out over who sleeps where."

Garrett waves that off. "I can shift and sleep on the end of someone's bed. I haven't been shifting enough lately anyway—it'll be good for me."

"I don't mind sharing," I volunteer. "Just let me send these to Hagen first."

Within fifteen minutes, the house is dark and silent as we all settle down, and I can't help the little thrill of excitement. Is this what having friends is like?

It's amazing.

ℳ

THE STRIDENT RING of my phone drags me awake not quite five hours later, and I groan as I roll over and grope for it. At the end of the bed, Garrett whines.

The time on the screen says it's just before seven. Hagen's name is also displayed there, and I find myself all the way awake very quickly.

"Hello?"

"Yeah, hi… sorry it took me so long, Jaid was in the mood to tease."

It takes me a minute to realize Jaid must be his boyfriend's name. Before I can think of an acceptable response, he's continuing.

"I've had a look through what you sent, and you're missing a full site survey. It's impossible for me to give a definite answer without that."

"A full site survey," I repeat. Garrett's ears prick up. "Okay, so no definites without a site survey, but if you had to give an opinion? Do you think it's worth getting a site survey?"

"Yes," he says immediately. "I looked up information from sites I think would be similar, and I'd absolutely recommend getting the survey. My money's on it showing that this is a viable project." He hesitates. "Expensive, though. Can you be sure you'll get a return on investment?"

"We think so." My thoughts are racing. I'm slightly distracted by how professional Hagen sounds—I don't know him well, but all week in the chat, he hasn't struck me as focused or serious. Now, though… if he's right, I don't know why Zac would have shelved the project. Could he have already gotten the site survey and it was just somewhere else? Or maybe he doesn't think the village can afford the startup costs?

"Thanks, Hagen. If I track down a site survey, I'll let you know." I do a mental calculation—it's late there. "I really appreciate you spending your Friday night on this."

"No problem. That's what support bros are for. Plus, the whole heist thing? Epic, man. I'm impressed."

I flush with pleasure and mumble my goodbyes. "Did you get all that?" I ask Garrett, and he shifts into his biped form.

"Yes. Sounds like we need to get a site survey."

"How, though? We're right back where we started—if we confront them without being sure it's a good idea, they'll stonewall us. And we can't just get a site survey without people wanting to know why."

Garrett's eyes narrow. "Just leave it to me."

<hr>

CHAPTER SIXTEEN

Zac

I WANDER into the kitchen and stop. At some point during my workout, our house apparently became the place to be.

"Hi," I say. "Is someone making breakfast?" It's the only reason I can think of for not only Micah and Cam, but also Zoe and Ronan to be here in the—now crowded—kitchen with Asher and Garrett.

"Breakfast would be good," Garrett says. "But that's not why we're here."

"It's not?"

"You live here," Asher reminds him.

I'm not sure what's going on, but I think pancakes are going to be needed. Bacon, too.

"I know I live here, Asher. I'm not an idiot." Garrett stops and takes a deep breath. "I'm sorry. I haven't had much sleep."

"About that," Micah interrupts, frowning. "Nobody told me movie night was going to be a sleepover. I was worried."

"It was part of your penance," Cam informs him. I have no idea what that means, but as Micah's cousin and brother in all but name, it's my job to enjoy moments like these.

Micah's brows draw together, and he looks at me, mouthing, "Penance?"

I shrug and get out the flour.

"Okay," Asher says in his reasonable oldest-cousin voice that always made me want to hit him, "Clearly there's something on your mind, and since you dragged Micah over here, too, I assume it's something you want to share with us all?"

Garrett smiles at him, and while Asher instantly relaxes and smiles back, something about it makes me suspicious. I try to look as busy as possible preparing the pancake batter while keeping an eye on everyone. Something is definitely going on.

"I need some help, actually. We," he gestures to his little posse, "were talking last night about what will happen when the museum's up and running. I know, I know, there's ages until then." He makes a wry face. "But you know I get excited about projects. And Ronan's finding some incredible stuff. I already know for sure we're going to have academics swarming the place."

Asher looks at Micah, who shrugs. "That's what we're hoping for, right?"

Garrett's gaggle all nod. It's… creepy.

"Yeah. And I know long-term plans are already in progress to add some hotels to the village, but that's going to take a while."

"We've talked about this," Micah reminds him. "Short-term, we can teleport academics in daily—or if you have an elf lined up to do portals, even better. We can easily set up accommodation for them in Zurich until the village is better equipped."

"Uh-huh." Garrett nods again. "I know, and while I

love that plan, I can't help thinking of all those tourism dollars lost. Plus, for as long as we're doing that, we're only going to be catering to academics. Not the family tourists we really want to attract to the town. The ones who might fall in love with the place and decide to move here to raise their kids."

I have a sudden, horrible feeling that he's going to bring up the ski resort again. Fuck. How am I going to blow it off this time?

"But there's nothing we can do," Micah's saying patiently. "Hotels take time to build, even small ones."

It's Zoe's turn to speak, and her voice is pure honeyed sympathy. "Yeah, and we know you've done so much work on getting the plans for them done so fast, Micah. Cam's told us how hard you've been working. We're just thinking… and this isn't a reflection on you *at all*… but there are designs for a medium-sized hotel and two small ones all worked up, right? Priced, approved, ready to start construction this summer?"

Micah nods warily. "Yes."

"Why aren't we thinking on a bigger scale?"

"Because the construction season here is short. We need to focus on getting the buildings to weatherproof stage before winter," Micah explains patiently. "And we can only get so many crews and supplies and equipment up here at a time. Even teleporting things in takes a lot of demons and effort."

"Um." Cam half raises his hand. "You're thinking like a demon."

Even I turn away from my pancake batter at that. He does know we're demons, right?

Under our bewildered stares, he shakes his head, curls flopping around. "What I mean is, you're thinking like a demon who's used to living in a secret village that nobody else comes to."

"It's not secret," Asher protests.

"And people come here," I add. "You're here. So are Garrett and Ronan and Zo—" I shut my mouth when I realize where he's going with this.

"Me?" Zoe smiles. "Yep. The sorcerer who specializes in snow manipulation."

My cousins and I look at each other, then Micah clears his throat. "Are there... sorcerers who specialize in construction? Who, if they were in a place that no humans had access to, could use their powers to build something a lot faster than usual? Just hypothetically."

"I might know some people who know some people." Zoe shrugs innocently.

"If we can get the hotels done faster, we should also think *bigger*," Garrett hurries on. "Instead of just a few hotels in the village, why aren't we looking at expanding? Maybe family-style self-catering accommodation behind the village? I know it's steep, that slope, but could we terrace it or something? Do the excavation work this summer while the other hotels are going up, prefab the cabins or whatever somewhere else, get them in next spring, and be open for at least part of the summer next year."

"The museum will be running by then," Ronan adds quietly. "And the first wave of academics will have been and gone, probably over the winter and spring. It would be an ideal time to show off the village."

"And," Zoe's excitement is clear, "winter is when this place could really *shine*. I can make it the ultimate snow fantasy. Kids will be begging to come here in winter—and it would be *safe* for them. No humans. They can show their horns or fangs and be faster or stronger than humans expect. It would be the same haven for them that it has been for everyone who lives here; except for them, it would be a true vacation. Not just relaxing, but no hiding. No pretending."

She does make it sound good. If I didn't already live here, I'd want to visit, just based on that pitch.

I check the pan on the stove, then ladle in the first lot of batter.

"It sounds like you've put a lot of thought into this," Asher says. "But it's not that easy. Like you said, the land behind the village is steep. We'd need to get some surveys done before any decisions could be made."

"That makes sense," Cam says—a little too quickly.

"It does," Garrett agrees. "Can we do that? Who do we need to hire for something like that?"

"There are companies that specialize in it. Micah? This is your field." Asher passes the ball neatly.

"I know some people," Micah says slowly. "But they couldn't do the survey with all this snow and the ground so frozen. It would be late spring before they could even begin, and then the reports would probably take a few weeks. I'm assuming you don't want to pitch it to the village council until you know it can be done?"

"Uh… yeah." Cam nods quickly. "Not until then. In fact, we don't want anyone to know except the people in this room."

I flip the pancakes. That's not suspicious at all. But at least the heat is off me. I try not to feel bitter that Garrett might get his family cabins while my resort is going to molder in my desk drawer.

"That's not possible," Asher's saying. "People are going to notice the surveyors."

I glance up in time to see the freaky four exchanging

glances. "There's no way to keep it secret?" Garrett asks. "And no way for the survey to be done sooner?"

Even Asher and Micah are getting suspicious now. The rose-tinted lenses of love don't make them completely stupid. "Why's it so urgent?"

"I want the village to diversify," Garrett says patiently. "That's the reason I came here, remember? The cave is *extra*. A bonus. A means to the end that is a fully integrated community here in Hortplatz. It's a long game, but that doesn't mean I can't stack the odds."

I put the first pancakes on a serving plate and add more batter to the pan, then turn and hand the plate to Ronan, who somehow has come up beside me. "Could you put this on the table?" I ask. "Grab one for yourself first, before the savages get them." There are no plates or condiments out, but hey, I cooked. They can set the table their own damn selves.

"Sure," he says, taking the plate, but he doesn't move. "Uh, I just wanted to say thanks. Again. For last night. I-I hope I can return the favor really soon and give you something you want."

My mouth goes dry. Did he feel what I did when he kissed my cheek? Is this him hinting that he'd be okay with more than professional friendship? Or is he genuinely just grateful for my help and offering to do something nice for me?

I swallow. Until I'm sure… I can't risk fucking up our relationship with the dragons. Not when we're still recovering from the last disaster. "Thanks. Uh… I'm glad I could help."

He smiles, and it's less wary than usual. I've only seen this smile a few times. It makes me think he spends a lot of time holding back, and this is the real him peeking through.

As he turns away with the plate, I tune back in to the conversation the others are still having. "You know," Micah's saying, "I'm pretty sure when we did the original surveys for the village, we included that area."

"Really?" Cam jumps forward to grab Micah's arm and nearly knocks Ronan over.

"Careful!" I snap, then grimace. "Sorry. Are you both okay?"

Cam gives me his usual sunny grin, but Ronan's smile is warmer. "Fine, thank you."

"Micah, do you still have those surveys?" Garrett asks. "And would they even be relevant to the kind of excavation we can do these days?"

Micah shrugs. "For the kind of thing you're talking about, they'd show if there was anything that would completely rule it out. If I remember right, we decided not to use it at the time because it was going to be a lot more expensive to build on that grade, and there was more than enough space for us on more level ground. But these days, with modern equipment, it would cost less to excavate— and if you're planning to make profit from the result, it's an investment, not an expense."

"Do. You. Still. Have. Them?" Garrett grinds out.

I turn away from the stove, and my surprise is amplified when I see the expressions on his and his friends' faces. For some reason, this is really important to them. Ronan looks like he's holding his breath, his face more intense than I've ever seen it.

Micah's completely taken aback. "Uh… maybe? They're probably in the village council's records. I might have a copy in my office. I can't promise, though—when we switched to electronic record-keeping, we threw out a lot of stuff."

"Did you scan the old stuff first?" Zoe asks. "Do you have the report in the cloud somewhere?"

He looks between them all, then turns a bewildered gaze on me and Asher. I shrug. Not getting involved with the rabid wolves.

"I can check?" he suggests.

They wait.

"Now. I'll, um, go check now."

Cam beams. "Aw, thank you. That's so sweet." He stands on tiptoe and kisses Micah smack on the mouth. "I'll be waiting right here for you to bring it back with you."

Micah leaves the kitchen, presumably to find his laptop, and I give all my attention to the pancakes. Whatever's going on here, it's got nothing to do with me.

CHAPTER SEVENTEEN

Ronan

THE WAIT for Micah to come back is agonizing. Trust me, I'd know. I've had quite a few agonizing waits in my life.

The wait to meet my brother... and then the belief that he'd betrayed me.

The wait for *him*—or anyone—to come back from battle. Followed by the realization that nobody was coming and I was now alone in a hostile world.

The wait for Brandt, for that incredible feeling of belonging, to come and see me in the prison cell. The wait for him to come back. The devastation of having everything I'd thought to be true crumble... and then the wait to finally meet my brother and begin a new life.

This should be nothing compared to all that, but somehow... it's not. I can't stop remembering Zac's voice on the phone when he thought I was hurt. His face as he patiently helped me through my "meltdown." The way he left his warm bed in the middle of a cold night to come to the aid of someone he doesn't really know... and even when he discovered what a fool's errand it was, stayed because he thought I needed him.

A man like that deserves everything he wants in life. If this ski resort is possible, there's nothing I won't do to make it happen for him.

We force ourselves to eat, partly because we're hungry but mostly because Zac makes a snide comment about not cooking just so the food can go cold. It's hard to concentrate on pancakes and bacon when so much is hanging in the balance. If this fails… well, I'll just have to find another way to show Zac how special he is. I need him to be my friend—I didn't realize how much until last night.

Suddenly, Garrett's head snaps around. "Is that the printer? Is he printing? Did he find it?" He starts to get up, but Asher plants a hand on his shoulder and pushes him back into the chair.

"Stay. If he found it, he'll bring it. If not, we'll go to the post office later and search the council records… and hope nobody wonders what we're doing there."

"We should go at night," Cam suggests conversationally. "The cover of darkness is best for things like that." He waves his fork, almost taking Zoe's eye out. "Last night, nobody even—"

The table jumps as three of us try to kick him at the same time. Zac, finished at the stove, takes a seat and gives Asher a wry look. "Do you get the feeling there's something we don't know?"

Asher's eyes are narrowed. "Oh, yeah."

Garrett sniffs. "I'm a hellhound of mystery."

"And I'm an incubus." Cam's smile is sunny, but there's a sudden edge to him that brings tension to the room. "Nobody asks for *all* my secrets, unless you want me to ask for yours."

Zoe shrugs. "You need me more than I need you. There's snow in lots of places."

As one, they turn to me. I freeze. "Uh… I just really

like it here. And I want friends." Oh, wait. "And if someone could get me a stand mixer with a dough hook attachment, that would be good. Because I saw this recipe for cinnamon rolls, and I think that would make it easier. And bread too."

Garrett turns on Asher so fast, I almost don't see his head move. "Get him the mixer. Go today." He looks at me. "Which one do you want? Do you have a color preference?"

I gape.

"Never mind. Asher, just get the best one they have. In all the colors. And every attachment."

"I'm really missing something," Asher mutters, and Zac laughs.

"Ronan likes to bake. I guess he was being modest yesterday when he told me about it."

"The pastries," Cam says dreamily. "I want all the pastries."

Zac's smile warms me from the inside. "I can go to Zurich later and get one for you."

He's being so nice, and guilt over all my lies last night floods through me. "I—"

"Found it," Micah announces, walking in with a handful of papers. Cam leaps up, kisses him, then snatches the papers and spreads them over the table, pushing aside plates and condiments. We all lean forward.

I bite back a groan. It's the same jargon as the other reports.

"Can any of you even understand that?" Micah's amused voice floats over our heads.

"Why don't you explain it to us?" Garrett asks.

Micah shrugs. "I don't know. You've been kind of demanding today, and there's definitely something going on that you're not telling us. Maybe we should discuss a trade of information."

"A trade sounds good," Cam agrees, surprising me. "How about this: if you don't tell us what all this means, it's going to be a long time before you next get to come." His curls flop endearingly into his wide eyes. "That's a fair trade, right?"

"There goes our leverage," Asher mumbles to Zac.

Sighing, Micah points to one page and begins an explanation of what it says. He's two sentences in when Zoe interrupts. "Could we have the tl;dr version, please?"

"What does that mean?" I ask. Normally I hate showing my ignorance, but I know I'm safe here. Last night proved that.

"Too long; didn't read."

I grin. I'll have to remember that one. Maybe later I can get her to explain what "that's what he said" means, because Dustin still hasn't.

"To summarize"—Micah sounds grumpy—"the land should be fine for the sort of project you have in mind."

Hope explodes in my stomach. "Really?" It comes out on a wispy breath.

"Yeah. I'd want an updated report before works actually begin, but based on this, I'd be happy to recommend the planning and scheduling could take place. There are a few issues this report highlights that wouldn't be relevant anymore, given modern machinery, and the costs would definitely be lower."

I look at my friends. Garrett's staring at me intently and drops his gaze toward… my lap?

Um…

"Do you need to…" His thumb wiggles.

Oh! He's wondering if we should send this report to

Hagen. I shake my head. "Micah knows what he's talking about."

"Thanks? I think." Micah shakes his head in bewilderment.

Cam stands abruptly, banging his hip on the table. "We need a secret conference. Come on."

That's a good idea. Zoe, Garrett, and I get up and follow him toward the living room. Garrett turns back in the doorway and glares at the demons. "Don't try to listen, or you'll regret it."

"Is it too early for a fucking drink?" I hear Asher ask as the door closes.

We crowd in a tight circle near the couch and keep our voices down.

"Well?" Zoe asks. "Now what do we do?"

"We need to find out why Zac shelved the project," Garrett says. "It seems completely viable to me. And a good idea. It's exactly the kind of thing we should be moving forward with."

"You really don't know why? Think hard," I urge. "Exactly what was said?"

Cam and Garrett exchange a long look. "Zac was looking at the papers," Cam says slowly. "Micah looked at some of them. He seemed to think it was a good idea, but I think he said something about a survey."

"Like Hagen did." I nod. "Okay, that makes sense."

Garrett chimes in. "Zac and Asher talked about it too. I wasn't there, but Ash mentioned it to me. He thought it would be a good part of our growth plan. I agreed. And then the next time I asked him about it, he said Zac shelved it."

"That was just a week later," Cam adds. "I remember because Micah was quiet. He wasn't sure if he should ask why. And Zac's been a grump since around then."

"Didn't you say last night that Cam brought it up at dinner last week?" Zoe asks. "What did Zac say then?"

"Damaris was on the warpath," Garrett says immediately. "From the minute we arrived. Dinner was awkward. Uh... Cam asked Zac about the plans. Zac said it was shelved. I asked why, I remember that. And that's when Damaris blew up about... that other stuff."

Cam shakes his head. He's frowning, and it looks oddly out of place on his usually cheerful face. "Didn't she say something about Zac not wasting time on dreams? It seemed like a really weird thing for her to say. And I'm sure he said something else about how the resort would be a good idea, but then she did her thing."

Certainty settles inside me. "Damaris is on the village council"—I know that for a fact—"and she played a huge part in the resettlement all those years ago, didn't she?" That's something I found out during my chats with the villagers.

"I wouldn't hesitate to say that she's the most influential person in the village," Garrett says grimly. "Even though this is officially Jesse's home, he's often away visiting other demons. And he frequently will defer to her about the village, since he knows she has its best interests at heart."

"So it's a safe bet that if Zac wanted to pitch this idea to the council, he'd have run it past his grandmother first?" Zoe sounds sad. "And she said no. So he shelved it."

"Fuck that." The words are louder than I expected, and I wince, lowering my voice again. "This is a good idea, right? We all think it can work?"

They murmur agreement.

"And Asher and Micah, they thought it could work?"

"Micah did," Cam says confidently.

"Asher was definitely intrigued," Garrett adds. "As a

business proposition, he was prepared to invest, subject to the land being usable."

"Which we now have the answer to. So we have two experts in agreement on this. Three, if you count Zoe as a winter sports expert. Four, with Garrett as the social anthropologist. Zac's the nature and wildlife expert—he never would have suggested this if it would cause problems there." Of that, I'm certain. "We need to find out what problem Damaris has with the idea and work out a solution."

"You want to confront Damaris Bailey?" Zoe pats my shoulder. "I'll give you a really nice eulogy."

"She won't dare," I say, newfound confidence surging through me. "It would be a diplomatic disaster." Plus, I'm not above using blackmail if I have to. Damaris owes me for keeping her secret, and I'm sure Garrett and the others have made sure she knows that.

If they haven't, I will.

"Even if we can face down Damaris, the second we do, *they'll* find out about it," Garrett says grimly, nodding toward the kitchen. "If we're going to do this, we're better off telling them first and having them with us."

Hearing that "we" warms my heart.

"Damaris might already have given Zac a reason," Cam points out reasonably. "If she has, we can find a solution, then go around her and present the idea to the whole council at once."

"I like that idea," I murmur. But... "It means we have to tell them what we did." Tell Zac that I lied to and stole from him. "He might refuse to talk about it after that."

Garrett looks thoughtful. "Asher and Micah will want answers. If Zac really, truly wants us to leave the project on the shelf, they'll back him, but I think once we tell them everything we know, they'll want to at least know what

Damaris said to him. He might not say it in front of us, but I bet they'll get it out of him."

"And if it's stupid, they'll tell him and find out if he wants their support." Cam nods. "That's the thing about these guys. They're always on the same side. If Zac wants the resort and it's doable, they'll back him on that too."

"I'm in," Zoe declares. "But I probably have the least to lose."

"Oh, I'm in." I surprise myself, but it's true. I want to make Zac happy again. I got a glimpse of smiley him the day I arrived—just for a second, when he wasn't being an ass to me—and people always talk about him being the fun one.

I want to give that back to him. I want him to smile at me.

Cam shrugs. "Micah will forgive me. So will Zac— we're friends. Friends sometimes do what's good for you whether you like it or not."

Garrett squints at him. "Have you been spending time with my cousin Alistair?" He shakes his head. "Never mind. Let's do this."

CHAPTER EIGHTEEN

Zac

"We did something," Garrett announces. The four of them marched back into the kitchen a moment ago and are now standing in a line, their faces determined. "You need to hear us out before you get mad."

"Well, that's reassuring," I murmur. Micah and Asher exchange glances. Truthfully, I'm kind of looking forward to this. Part of me has seen how happy my cousins are with their men and been a little envious, but at moments like this, I get to point and laugh while they deal with the fallout.

"What did you do?" Micah asks.

Cam lifts his chin. "I will *not* be treated as anything but an equal partner, Micah. You don't get to declare that something isn't up for discussion if I want to discuss it."

Micah blinks, then his jaw drops. "This is about —that?"

"I had questions. They were valid. It's a subject that affects us and our life here. Right, Garrett?"

Whoa. So this *isn't* about Cam and Micah?

Garrett nods. "Exactly. I also had questions about something that affected not only my marriage and home, but the job I was hired to do here. I don't appreciate being brushed off."

Asher darts a glance at me. "There wasn't anything more to be said."

Folding his arms, Garrett lifts his chin. "We disagree. We discussed it," he gestures to the other three, "and decided we needed more information."

I still don't know what they're talking about, but it sounds like we're getting to the good bit.

"Which is why we broke into Zac's room and stole the plans for the ski resort."

Shock hits me like a freight train, and all enjoyment drops away. "You did what?" My gaze goes to Ronan, to the guilt plastered on his face.

"It was my idea," he blurts. "I planned it all and then I lied to you. You were so kind, and I deceived you. I'm sorry. But Cam and Garrett said you'd been excited about the ski resort, and I wanted to give you something that would make you happy. I want you to like me." The last words are wobbly, but he squares his shoulders. "We stole the plans from your room. The business idea is viable, and Zoe and Garrett both think it's what the village needs. I asked a friend to look at the rest of it, and he said it looked feasible but depended on the results of a site survey." He points at the papers on the table. "That site survey says it would be fine. So the only reason we can think of that you would have shelved this project that made you happy before is that you talked to Damaris about it, and she said no. But she's wrong."

I fold my arms to hide the way my hands are shaking. How is this happening? "I'm not talking about this."

Ronan shrugs. "That's fine. But unless you have another reason for shelving the project, we plan to take this whole thing to the village council." He sets his jaw. "Your grandmother won't say no to me."

The room is so quiet, I hear Zoe's clothes rustle as she leans over to whisper to Cam, "Is this turning you on too?"

"Kind of," he whispers back, staring at Ronan. "We should have befriended him sooner."

"I can hear you," Ronan says, but his eyes are locked with mine. "It's your call, Zac. You come with us and claim ownership of this like you deserve, or we do it anyway. Either way, I'm not letting a good man get kicked for no reason. Not ever again." The bitter vehemence in his voice cuts through my shock and anger.

"To be clear, you lied to me and made me worry about you, then you violated my privacy and robbed me," I summarize, "and now you want me to believe it was for my own good?" I take a step closer to him. "Are you sure this isn't just revenge? I was an ass to you, and now you want to humiliate me too?"

He looks like I've struck him, and I hate myself for saying those words. Whatever fragile beginnings of friendship might have been between us couldn't have survived them.

To my surprise, he lifts his chin. "When I met you, you smiled and introduced yourself and were happy. Everyone here says you're a nice person. A happy person. A fun person. I've rarely seen that side of you. Partly that's my fault, but not all of it. And if we're right, someone else did that to you. Made you a person who isn't happy. Made you a different person than who you really are. Nobody should be allowed to do that."

I can't breathe. There's something going on here, more

than just me being unhappy about my ski resort. "Why do you care?" It's barely a whisper.

He looks away. The ticking of the clock in the living room seems to echo through the whole house.

Ronan closes the distance between us, grabs my shoulders, and plants a kiss on my mouth. It's awkward. My lip smashes against a tooth. It's over in a heartbeat. But the electricity that sparked between us…

I swallow dryly as he steps back. "I'm sorry. I shouldn't have done that. I don't… I guess I probably won't see you again after this, and I just wanted…" He shakes his head. "The longer you're someone different, the harder it is to get back to who you really are, Zac. I don't know why you let your grandmother bully you. Any of you." His glance takes in Asher and Micah, and I hear an indrawn breath but can't look away from Ronan. "The thing is, people who love you should love you even when you tell them no. If they don't, they never loved you at all. You shouldn't have to always please them."

He turns around and faces Garrett, Cam, and Zoe, who are still and pale. "I'm sorry. I ruined it. The resort's a good idea, and it's what the village needs. I can make sure Damaris doesn't cause trouble. But I think maybe it's better if that's the only part I play. And… and I'll call Brandt and have him find an elf at the DEA who can portal me to the cave every day. Nobody needs to be uncomfortable because of me."

He's halfway to the door before my wits come back.

"Wait." My voice is hoarse, and I cough. "Ronan, wait."

He stops and turns around, but now I don't know what to say. It's pretty obvious that someone hurt him, someone he thought he could trust. I need to step carefully around that, but right now I feel raw. In such a short time, with so little personal contact with any of us, he's somehow seen through us all. He was right about everything he said.

Everything.

His lower lip trembles, just the tiniest bit, and I shove aside my insecurities. He put himself out there for me—how can I not do the same?

Just like he did, I close the distance between us. I don't put my hands on him, though, just lean in and kiss him gently. "We can talk about this later," I whisper. "But nobody here is uncomfortable because of you. And if they are, they're the ones who can leave."

He's shaking, and when he raises his eyes to look at me, they're glossy with tears. His throat works, but he only nods.

"Okay." I turn to face my cousins. "Ask me about the ski resort."

Asher's face is stone; Micah's is thunder. But when he speaks, his voice is ice. "Why did you shelve the project?"

"The day after I talked to you about it, the day after Ronan arrived, I took the plans to Grandmother for her opinion. I knew that if she championed it, the council would approve it without question. I also thought it would be a good investment for our family." I pause. The memory of her words still cuts me; saying them aloud won't be easy. "She didn't even listen. I said I had an idea for a ski resort, and she told me to stop wasting time on dreams, because the village needed me to do my duty. So I shelved the project."

Asher snarls. "You've always done your duty. We all have. Our whole lives are built around our duties to this village."

"Asher," Garrett murmurs, going to him, but Asher shakes his head.

"No. We say it's fine because she let us all come and go for our studies and travel and choose the careers we wanted, and we all get to work in fields we love, but it's *not* fine that Micah is expected to shuffle his own clients to fit in work for the village—unpaid. And it's *not* fine that in any other town in the world, the work Zac does would require a team of people, and yet here he's not even an official employee of the village. If he didn't have family money to support himself with—that I'm required to manage—he'd be fucked. Yet even with all that, she waves the word 'duty' around and announces that we'll help out with all these extra projects. I'm done. I'm done with her thinking she owns us. Maybe I could put up with the rest of it and the matchmaking, because I convinced myself she had good intentions, but to not even listen to Zac, her grandson? Not even listen? No. I'm done." He hauls his phone out of his pocket.

"Who are you calling?" Garrett asks in alarm.

"Gideon." His thumb slides up the screen, scrolling.

"Why?"

Asher looks up. "Why? I'm telling a representative of CSG exactly what Grandmother did in the cave. I'm telling him everything else too. We cover for her, and she thinks she can get away with it, so she does it again. She's been doing it for centuries, and people let it slide every time. Not anymore."

Garrett snatches the phone from his hands and dances out of his reach. "No."

Jaw dropped, Asher stares at him.

"Garrett's right," Ronan says. He sounds more composed now. "I don't know the full story here—matchmaking and your jobs and the rest of it. I know she volunteers you for things, and I know your family runs on her whim. But you can't report her to Gideon—this is Gideon Bailey? Your cousin?"

"Yes," I murmur. "Why can't we report her?" Because I can't lie, right now, I really want to. My resort is a viable idea, and she never even let me tell her about it. Asher's right—it's time to be done.

"First, because it's not your place. It's mine. For this to have the most impact, the report would need to come from me—or Garrett. It would also need to be made officially, not in an angry phone call to a relative. Second, the minute you report this, we lose our leverage over Damaris. Right now, I can make her agree to anything I want."

"I don't know." Cam pulls a face. "She's pretty strong-willed."

Ronan's smile is one I've never seen on his face before. It's not his hesitant social one or the genuine one that peeks through sometimes. This is hard and mean and speaks of a background I know nothing about. "I *will* make her agree."

There's a tiny silence as we all digest that, and Asher's face relaxes a tiny bit.

"And third," Ronan continues calmly, as though he didn't just claim he could take on the scariest woman alive, "if a report goes through and the consequences are what you said they would be, the village council is going to be in disarray. Getting approval for anything out of them will be that much harder."

"Um." Zoe half raises her hand. "I'm pretty sure I'm not supposed to know anything about whatever you're talking about, so I can just go away for a while and come back later?"

Shit. I forgot that part.

"Can we trust you?" Garrett asks, and Micah sucks in a

breath. I get it—this secret has the power to ruin our grandmother and potentially our whole family.

"Yes." Zoe's answer is firm and without hesitation. "I'll swear it on anything. I'm Team… whatever team this is."

We all look at Asher. He's the oldest. He's the one who was ready to burn everything to the ground a minute ago.

He nods. "Then let's make a plan."

CHAPTER NINETEEN

Ronan

AFTER A LONG DAY of planning and research and a snowball fight on Saturday, I fell into bed exhausted, convinced I'd be asleep the moment my head touched the pillow.

I was wrong.

Instead, I tossed and turned, sleeping fitfully in short, dream-laden bursts before finally giving up in the quiet hour before dawn. After two nights of poor sleep, I'm surprised my brain can even function, but in fact, it's churning at a million miles. I lie cocooned in my bed and stare up at the dark ceiling. Despite the many plans we made yesterday and the busy day—days, weeks, months—that lies ahead, all I can really think of is one thing.

One person.

Zac.

I'm not sure when he became more than just my liaison and guide. More than just someone I wanted to befriend. When I think about it, the immediate answer is "always," but if that's the case, why wasn't it obvious to me from the beginning? Some deep-down sense of self-preservation, maybe. The instinctive need to maintain whatever distance possible from a man who could tear apart my control.

Because there's no disputing that it's gone.

Any last vestige of the years—millennia—of training and instruction and brainwashing that *he* drilled into me has finally been ripped away. It's been fading for a long time, bit by bit, in tiny pieces, but… part of me didn't want to let it go. There's comfort and safety in the familiar, even when it hurts. Even when it's not good for you. Even when the whole point of it is to make you someone different.

And while the love and support my dragon family has given has helped me, I've never felt confident or secure enough to fully leave the past that imprisoned me behind.

Not until I saw Zac submitting to his own prison. Beautiful, strong, kind Zac, who gives of his time and self with no qualms. Whose love for his family and people is unquestioning. Who looked me in the eye and admitted he was wrong and apologized without excuse. Zac, who I've been drawn to from the first moment he flashed his bearded smile.

Zac, who I could never dream of being with unless we both smashed the chains binding us.

What I did Friday night and yesterday was selfish. The others might think different, but it was. Yes, the ski resort is a good idea and will be good for the village. Yes, I want Zac to be happy—to repay some of his kindness. But I want to be happy too. I want to be happy with Zac. And so I smashed their family to pieces.

Do I think it will be better for them all, healthier, in the long run? Yes. I honestly believe that. Bringing this out into the open will be good for the Baileys.

It would be hypocritical of me not to do the same.

I roll over, grab my phone, and do a quick time zone

calculation. Then I sit up, pile the pillows behind me, and make the call.

"If you're in danger, this line isn't secure," my brother answers. Affection wells up in me. When I was young, I loved the idea of him, an idea that was pure fiction. As I got older, I hated that same idea. We were strangers who shared the same face when we met, and though we know each other now, I don't know what our relationship is.

"I'm not in danger," I tell him. "But I do need to speak with you. It's important but not urgent, and I'd like it to be a private conversation." I keep my voice calm. Steffen's paranoia has been better and better over the years, but it reacts to strong emotion. I need to talk to my brother, not his trauma.

He pauses. "Give me a moment."

I hear some sounds in the background, low voices, and then a door closing.

"I'm here," Steffen says. "I'm alone. And the line is as secure as I can make it."

I smile involuntarily. Of course he'd care about that. "Ideally, I'd prefer to have this conversation in person, but that's not possible right now. Mostly because I think if I waited any longer, I'd lose my nerve."

"Are you sure you aren't in trouble?"

"I swear I'm not. Not the kind you mean. But I've been having some… emotional difficulties. For a long time now."

There's an uncomfortable hesitation. "I'm not the best person to talk to about emotions."

I answer his honesty in kind. "I know." It might be blunt, but anything else would be a lie. Lying to Steffen is stupid. "But this involves you. And… I think you might be the only person who could possibly relate in any way."

Another pause. "You're talking about Éibhear."

I flinch. I don't often do that anymore, but hearing *his* name now, when everything feels so exposed… "Yes. But mostly about after."

"After?"

It's my turn to hesitate, to weigh my words. "Our experiences with him were different. Very different. I'm not even going to pretend I can understand what you went through." I don't know the details. Steffen doesn't talk about it—not to me, anyway. All I know is that he was tortured from before he can remember until the day, hundreds of years later, when Wil and Brandt rescued him. It was during those years that his paranoia formed, a trauma response in his brain designed to protect him as much as possible from his tormentors. "But we both had our magic bound. We both grew up not knowing what it truly meant to be a dragon. After… how long did it take you to feel that you were one?"

"You *are* a dragon, Ronan," he growls, cutting straight to the point. "Has someone—"

"This isn't about anyone else, Steffen. Please listen to me. I know I'm a dragon, and I mourn for all those years of self that I lost. But… sometimes I feel like there's a different me inside. I feel like all those years with… with Éibhear, with him raising me to fit his own mold, changed me so much, I'm still not the person I was meant to be. I-I feel like I don't truly fit in with other dragons. That I don't belong."

I can hear him breathing, steady and sure, but for a long time, he says nothing. "I will never truly be the person I was meant to be." The words fall like stones between us, and I wince as I realize how insensitive I'm being. "That doesn't mean the person I am isn't me. To answer your question, it took me a long time to feel like a dragon. A lot longer than it's been for you. It… You've come further in finding yourself in these few years than I did in centuries." He stops, and I take an unsteady breath.

"I'm sorry. This was cruel of me. I—"

"I haven't helped you," he interrupts. "I… This conversation is about honesty, yes? When we discovered you existed, I didn't want you in my life. I didn't want a brother. I didn't want anything to remind me of… everything."

It's a knife strike, but not surprising. And I can't blame him.

"I was wrong about that," he continues, and that *does* surprise me. "I know I haven't been the brother you hoped for, but I'm glad to have you in my life. I mourn the time we lost, and that we never got to play together as children do."

"So do I." It's barely a whisper.

"What's brought this on?" he asks. "What happened?"

"There's a man here. His family… It's not like what happened to us. They love him, but the shackles are just as real. I-I wanted him to shake them off and live his dreams, but… then I realized, how can I tell him to do that when I'm not doing the same? I'm tired of being afraid that the wrong step will take it all away, Steffen. I want to be me."

"He's special to you."

"Yes." The answer falls naturally from my lips.

"Does he feel the same way?"

I think about it, about the soft way Zac kissed me and the way he asked last night if he could visit me this morning. "Possibly. It's early. And we're both dealing with other pressures."

"Nobody's taking it all away, Ronan. I understand that fear; I had it for so long. But dragons are forever true. Our whole species would need to be dust before we let you be torn from us."

He doesn't get it. "It's not the others I'm worried about, Steffen. It's you."

The sharp inhale is one of the biggest signs of emotion I've ever known him to give. "Me?"

"You didn't want a brother. I… I knew. Maybe I didn't admit it to myself, but I did know. I've tried so hard to build a bond with you. I understand why it's difficult for you, and I tried to never push. But I worry that one day, I'll do something that will cause you to walk away. It won't matter that there are still thousands of other dragons. I won't have my brother." The last word shakes, and I swallow hard. Steffen lives by rules. He has to. Safety and security are his highest priorities. I understand that, and why. I even respect it. The way his brain works has saved a lot of people's lives. But I don't think I can live that way forever. The dragon in me needs more.

"What could you do that you worry would make me walk away?"

I take a moment, then decide to go for it. "Well, what would you say if I told you that on Friday night, I masterminded a plot to lure a man from his home so my friends could sneak in and steal from him?"

"You did *what*?" His shock is expected, but still concerns me. "You've actually managed to surprise me. What did you steal, and why?"

I launch into the explanation, realizing only after I've had to backtrack a few times exactly how complicated it is. When I finally peter out, I brace myself.

"Ronan…"

Here it comes.

"You are *such* a dragon."

What? "I… am?"

"This is exactly the kind of story I would expect to

hear from Dustin or Fabian—though his version would include him having sex with the man."

"So… you're not angry? You don't want me out of your life?"

There's a long pause. "I *am* angry," he admits at last. "I'm angry because there are a thousand different things that could have gone wrong and put you in danger, and my brain calculated every single one of them while you told me that story. I'm angry because you're planning to face down a woman who even I would hesitate to go head-to-head with." I bite my lip, grateful I held back the part about blackmailing her. "But the rest? You doing something outlandish so somebody else can be happy? You taking steps to win the man you could love? I could never cut you out of my life for that. Although," he adds, "I'm going to lecture you about it. And now that I think of it, I'm going to come out there soon and check the security on your house. I don't like this idea that the demons can just teleport inside. I'm bringing you some weapons."

"Steffen." It's the barest whisper, but he hears it.

"Ronan. We didn't get the start we should have. And maybe neither of us will ever truly be the people we could have been if we'd grown up safe among dragons. But I will never, ever hate you for embracing your dragon nature. I want that for you. I want that for me, and maybe someday, I'll heal enough for it to happen. But you don't have to worry about losing me because of who you are."

"Thank you." I can tell he means it, and I'm grateful, but still a part of me doubts, and I blink back tears. I'd hoped this conversation would set my fears to rest, one way or another, but instead it seems they'll always haunt me.

"I want to tell you something," he says abruptly. "I… There are only ten people in the world who know this. It's my deepest secret. I want you to know. You're my brother, and I trust you with this. I trust that you would never betray me, because I know who you are, at your core."

I still, afraid to breathe.

"I've been in a relationship with Wil for four thousand years. He's the love of my life, and I'm afraid every day that someone will use that love against us both."

Memory rises of that day in Steffen's office—Wil's office—at DEA headquarters. The day they first learned I existed. The day I broke in and tried to hack Steffen's computer. And I imagine how he must have felt, knowing that someone who loathed him so much—because I did loathe him them—was mere feet away from the one person who meant everything to him. If I had known then, I would have used that against him. I would have made it a weapon to end him.

That he trusts me with it now is… everything. "I'll take this to my grave," I swear, my voice hoarse. "Nobody will ever hear it from me. Thank you for… Thank you." Tears stream from my eyes.

"Wil's going to be pleased I told you," he admits. "He wants us to be closer. I want that too. Even if you're going to be a reckless, unhinged plotter of a dragon."

The last of my fears fall away, and I'm free.

CHAPTER TWENTY

Zac

DESPITE THE FACT that I've been teleporting into Ronan's house all week, today I decide to walk over and use the front door. Things feel different now. Maybe it's old-fashioned of me, but I want to be formal about this.

I'm cursing myself as I walk up the front path. It's not old-fashioned, it's stupid, but I'm here now. Hopefully Ronan will understand why I didn't teleport, because I'm not sure I can explain it. Ringing the bell, I take a step back and try not to dwell on how weird it is that just one week ago, I was standing here, preparing to apologize and ask for a truce. And now…

The door opens, and my mouth involuntarily curls into a smile as Ronan appears… and then that smile vanishes as rage surges through me. "Who made you cry?" I demand, stepping forward and tipping his chin to the light. His eyes are faintly red-rimmed and slightly puffy. "Are you hurt?"

To my surprise, he smiles radiantly and throws his arms around me, squeezing tight. It only takes me a second to hug him back—his body pressed to mine feels too good to pass up, even through my thick parka.

Then he pulls back and takes my hand. "Come inside. You'll freeze." He's still grinning.

Obediently, I follow him, stripping off my outer gear and absently noting how good the house smells as he closes the door. "You're okay?" I ask, wanting to be certain, even though it seems like he is.

He nods as he leads me down the hall into the kitchen. The aroma of fresh baking is stronger here, the room cozily warmed by the heat of the oven. I can see something that looks like bread inside, and there are muffins cooling on a rack and a plate of cookies on the table. "You've had a busy morning." My mouth waters as I stare at the cookies.

Ronan's chuckle is like music. I haven't heard him laugh enough, and I want to hear it more... and frequently. I want to make him laugh. This sudden rush of feeling is so surreal to me. How can I have disliked him last week and now want him? Were my cousins that right about my head being up my ass?

"I had some thinking to do," he said, "and baking is cathartic. Sit and have a cookie. Do you want some tea? I've just boiled the kettle."

I'm more of a coffee drinker, but I don't mind tea. And the cookie's the important part. So I say, "Yes, please," then sit at the table and watch as he bustles around, spooning loose-leaf tea into a pot and carefully pouring boiling water over it. I haven't seen tea made that way in about a century. I guess tea bags are more convenient, but there is something nice about the ritual of making it this way.

He brings the pot and two mugs over to the table and takes the seat across from me. "It just needs a few minutes to steep." His hand reaches out to nudge the cookies closer to me. That's a hint I'm happy to take, so I grab one and bite in. Chocolate, cinnamon, and vanilla explode in my mouth, and the moan takes me by surprise.

Ronan's gaze is anxious on my face. "Good?"

I nod, too busy cramming in more cookie to speak, and he grins again, taking one for himself. Trying not to make it obvious that I'm staring, I take in every detail of his face. He's been crying, yes, but he also looks… happy. Peaceful? There's a sense of calm about him that I've never seen before. Since he got to Hortplatz, he's been tense and stressed. Even this past week, when things were better, there was still this air of… something. Like he was haunted. It's not completely gone, but it's better.

Swallowing, I say, "So… catharsis?"

He nods, checks the teapot, and then pours the hot liquid into the mugs. "After yesterday… well, I think it was obvious that I have some unresolved issues. Although to be fair, it was probably obvious before that too. So this morning I called my brother."

His twin—the one Gideon told us to step carefully around. "Are you close? Being twins and all."

His shake of the head is accompanied by a grimace. "We will be, I think. We're working on it. Things have been… difficult between us. Some of that was my fault, though I didn't know at the time…" He shakes his head again. "I can't tell you all of it. I'm sorry. But we were separated at birth and raised very differently. We only met again five years ago, and that was under bad circumstances." Guilt chases across his face. "We'd come to an understanding, but I always worried…" He sighs. "It's so complicated. Can we talk about this another time?"

"Of course," I agree, even though I'm dying to know more. He and his twin were separated? And for some reason, it seems like Ronan feels he's to blame for that? "As long as you're okay."

His smile comes back, softer this time. "I am. We had a good talk, and I'm more confident in our relationship now. Then I got to pound some bread dough and cry out the rest of my frustrations." He shoots a wry look toward the oven. "So if the bread tastes salty, that's why."

I laugh, reaching across the table to take his hand and twine my fingers with his. The warmth of his hand and smooth slide of his skin on mine sends tingles through me. Leaning forward, I lift our joined hands and kiss his fingers, and he jerks in my hold, a wave of pink rising in his face. I start to pull back, wondering if I misread things.

He holds on tight. "I'm bad at this," he babbles. "You probably guessed already. I-I don't have much experience —I mean, I was sheltered—and then…" He trails off, mouth turning down in frustration. "Please don't hate me."

Anger stirs again. "I don't hate you." I keep my voice as level as I can, but he's staring miserably at the tabletop, still clutching my hand like he's afraid I'll leave if he lets go. "Ronan, look at me."

Inhaling deeply, he raises his gaze to mine. It's uncertain, and I don't want him feeling that way about me. Not ever.

"I don't hate you," I repeat firmly. "And I don't care how inexperienced you are. You're safe with me—we can go as slow as you need to. I guess… I just want to know if this is something you want. With me, I mean. Things have been… Well, it's not like the beginning of this, us, has been all that conventional. We've both been distracted by other things in our lives. I think I'm safe in saying we didn't see each other clearly at first."

Some of the uncertainty clears, and he nods. "I wasn't seeing anything clearly. I…" He clears his throat.

"I wasn't raised by dragons. An elf raised me. And I-I didn't know much about dragons or my heritage until five years ago. I still sometimes feel like I don't fit in. So being here as a representative of dragons when I wasn't sure if I really was one..." He trails off and winces. "I felt like a fraud. And it was like salt in a wound—like I was being taunted for everything I don't know yet. Except Brandt would never do that, and then I felt guilty for even thinking it." He shakes his head. "It's been confusing."

I take a second to digest that. There are a lot of questions I want to ask, but I'm not going to push him… except on one thing. "Were you mistreated? By the elf who raised you?"

"No. Yes." He sighs and looks back at the table. "Not how you mean. He never beat me or anything like that. I had the best of everything. If you'd asked me even ten years ago, I would have said I had the best childhood anyone could have."

I wait, and his grip tightens on mine until it's painful. When his eyes lift again, they're glassy with tears.

"He bound my magic. My dragon. I-I couldn't shift until after I met Brandt… and I didn't even know what he'd done. Didn't know what I'd been missing for thousands of years."

Thousands? Pushing the thought aside, I cover our joined hands with my other one. "He mistreated you." I can't imagine having my innate demon self stifled. It makes my grandmother's bullying trivial—though it does clarify his strong feelings about it.

"I suppose." He seems reluctant to concede that. "I mean, he did… but not like… It could have been worse." He sighs again. "I can't talk about it. I'm sorry, I can't."

Something in the way he says that niggles at my brain,

but it's not important right now. All that matters is that he's okay.

"You *are* a dragon," I say quietly. "It doesn't matter that it was stolen from you before, or that you don't know all the things other dragons your age do. You're still a dragon."

He gives me a watery kind of smile, and the peace I saw earlier is back. "I know. This week has made me see a lot of things more clearly." He seems to realize how tight he's still holding my hand, because his grip suddenly loosens. "Sorry."

"Nope." I shake my head. "No apologies. Yesterday, you were there for me in a way I didn't know I needed someone to be." He's been open and honest with me today, and now it's my turn. "I've been so bitter lately, and I was just letting it happen. Even though I knew I had people who would be on my side. You made me *see* things. And no matter what ends up happening between us, my hand is always going to be here for you to hold when you need it."

"Thank you." He chews on his lip for a moment, and I try not to think about soothing the abused flesh with my tongue. "So... I would like for something to happen between us."

I grin. "Me too. And like I said, we can go slow. Whatever you're comfortable with." He said he was sheltered—I have to wonder if that means the elf who raised him kept him isolated. No wonder he struggled to connect with others in the village. "We can just date for a while."

He swallows. "I, uh. I know I wasn't very good at it, but I liked kissing you yesterday."

Without letting go of his hand, I get up and move to the chair beside him. My free hand lifts to cup his face. "Weren't good at it? It felt like I'd been electrocuted," I tease. "I liked kissing you too."

Those must be the magic words, because his nervousness drops away. "Maybe we should do some more kissing," he suggests. "Practice for me. It would be a huge favor." His mouth twitches in a tiny smirk. "I'd owe you."

"Owe me, huh? Could I have payment in cookies?"

An eyebrow shoots up. "Cookies? That's a pretty steep price. I'm going to need some proof that you're worth it." His eyes widen in horror. "That's not what I meant! Of course you're worth cookies. I was just… ugh. I was trying to be cute and I *failed*."

I laugh. "You didn't fail. You flirted with me, and it worked. I'm totally at your mercy. One sample kiss coming right up." Before he can protest, I lean in and capture his lips. The bottom one is puffy from being bitten, and he tastes like chocolate and cinnamon and something uniquely *him*, but I barely notice any of that because of the same electric sensation that struck me yesterday. Twice.

Kissing him is going to be addictive.

CHAPTER TWENTY-ONE

Ronan

I'M GRINNING when I open my front door for Zoe that evening. The smile hasn't left my face all day... except for when my lips were pressed to Zac's. And that was a lot.

A *whole* lot.

Most of the day, actually.

Kissing Zac is my favorite thing to do, ever. I haven't been kissed much before, but it was nothing like when Zac and I kiss.

We kissed in the kitchen. Then the oven timer interrupted us, and after I took the bread out, I dragged him to the living room, where we kissed some more in between me thanking him for the new stand mixer he bought me yesterday.

We kissed over a lunch of sandwiches and muffins.

We kissed while talking about his plans for the ski resort. He's so excited about it, and I can't wait to help him make it happen.

We kissed when I confessed that the group chat is actually a "help Ronan make friends" group, and that they finally settled on the weird name of "Ro Ro Ro The

Group." Zac laughed so hard, he choked, then explained that it's probably a pun on a children's nursery rhyme about a boat. He sang it to me, and I kissed him again.

In fact, we kissed right up until he had to drag himself away for family dinner, leaving me just enough time to daydream and get ready for Zoe to collect me. The plan we made yesterday was to speak to Damaris as a group after dinner was done, but before her children left the house. Garrett and Zoe were sad that the cousins felt the need to have their parents nearby as witnesses, but I get it. Damaris may have been doing what she genuinely believed is right, but that doesn't mean she gets to control her family like this. They won't see that until it's shoved in their faces.

"Someone's had a good day," Zoe says, wiggling her brows. "I wonder why that could be?"

My face gets hot. "Shut up. No, wait—how did you know?"

She laughs. "Ronan, your lips look like a blowfish's and there are stars in your eyes. If this was a cartoon, there would be little pink hearts circling your head. Either you had a good day with Zac or you and your vacuum cleaner have an unhealthy relationship."

I snort. "That's disgusting. Do you want to come in?"

"We don't have time." She motions for me to hurry up. "Get a coat if you're still pretending to need one, and you can tell me everything on the way over there."

I ignore the jibe about pretending to need a coat and get one. I'm still trying to fit in here. Then I pull the door shut and link my arm with hers. It's strange to think that we only met properly a week ago, and yet I'm this comfortable with her in my personal space.

"Soooooo?" she asks. "How was it?"

"I'm not giving you details," I warn, glad that the night helps to hide the flush of color on my face. Not that there are a lot of details. We kissed. And felt each other up a bit —through our clothes.

"Yeah, not asking for them. But," she side-eyes me, "are you guys… you know. Together? Dating? Hooking up? Thinking about any of the above?"

I hesitate. This situation is completely foreign to me. "I guess we're dating. But we're taking it slow. I… Well, making friends isn't the only thing I don't have a lot of experience with." I avoid looking at her while I say it, but she squeezes my arm.

"Sweetie, you just needed some practice with the friend-making. Look at you now! You have three new friends who like you so much they committed a crime with you, *and* you've been inducted into a bigger friendship circle with their significant others."

I blink. "I have?"

"Pfft. Do you think guys like Asher and Micah would have let you be part of all this if they didn't consider you at least friend-adjacent?"

Hmm. "I don't think I really gave them a choice. After I robbed their cousin and told them all that their grandmother's a bully I plan to blackmail, I was kind of in the middle of it."

"Fine, don't believe me. But they would have found a way to keep you out of it tonight if they didn't trust you. Besides, now you and Zac are dating, so you're almost part of the family. That's another thing you achieved this week —you turned a maybe-truce into a maybe-boyfriend. With enough time, you could probably take over the world."

I shudder hard. It's completely involuntary, her words triggering the worst of memories, and it's noticeable enough that she stops walking. "Ronan? What's wrong?"

A smile is beyond me, but I manage to swallow down the bile that's filled my mouth. "Nothing. Just… don't joke about that, okay? Taking over the world. It's…" I can't tell her the truth, not all of it, just like I couldn't tell Zac. The fact that *he* planned to take over the world and enslave all its peoples is highly classified, and my role in it is still something I'm ashamed of, even though I was brainwashed my whole life. "I was raised by a megalomaniac, and I have some PTSD."

She hugs me, right there in the middle of the street. "I'm sorry. I swear, no more jokes like that. Just be proud of what you're achieving, okay?"

The combination of her confidence in me and the hug warm me all the way to my toes. "I am," I admit, then say it again, more firmly. "I am. And now I'm going to threaten an old woman and make her cower before me."

Zoe snorts as we start walking again. "Out of context, that doesn't make you sound like a hero."

"Even good guys need to do bad things sometimes," I inform her. "And it's not like I'm actually hurting anyone. She won't suffer because of this. I'm just going to bruise her ego a little."

"True. But, getting back to what we were saying before… I'm not sure how much experience you don't have, but I want you to know, I'll help if you have questions. Though gay sex isn't my area of expertise, so you might be better off with Cam."

As much as I appreciate the matter-of-fact way she says it, I still want to die right now. I'm literally thousands of years older than any of them, and yet she can tell I need sex tips. Because she's right—I have very little idea what I'm doing. I told her and Zac that I don't have a lot of experience, but the truth is, I'm a virgin. A few experimental kisses and today's blissful encounter with Zac are all I've ever done.

The thought of having to explain that to her, or to

Cam, an incubus for whom sex is second nature, makes all my newfound confidence wither.

"Thank you," I say. She's being supportive.

"And you can always talk to Zac," she adds. "You said he was happy to take things slow, right?"

I think about how gentle and patient Zac is, and how when things started to get really heated, he made himself stop to check if I was okay with it, and my concern melts. "He's perfect."

"Ugh, gag. Okay, new rule: I'm thrilled and supportive of your relationship and happy to talk about it, but only if you don't gush over how amazing Zac is."

Laughing, I stick out a hand for her to shake as we stop in front of Damaris's house. "Deal."

"Good. Now, before we beard the lioness in her den, I just want to go on record that last week I thought you and Zac would be a great couple and I was totally planning to push you together."

I think back to the things she added to my list. "Is that why you wrote that he's hot as fuck?"

She winks. "You bet."

Cam's the one who opens the door to us, and he grins wide. "Great job, Ronan! The beard burn on Zac's neck is impressive."

My face gets hot again. "Oh no. Is it that obvious?"

He shrugs. "I was looking for it, so maybe not to everyone. You're just lucky he has a beard, or both of you would look like you have sunburned faces. I can give you a recipe for some lip balm that will bring that swelling down, by the way. It really helps."

"Thank you," I manage weakly, trying not to think about the fact that I'm about to face Zac's whole family with my mouth all swollen from his kisses.

"Come in. We're in the living room, and Asher just told

the kids to go play with the toys he and Zac bought them when they got your stand mixer."

They're ready to start, then. Zoe and I strip off our outer layers, hang them neatly by the door, and follow Cam.

"…very mysteriously," a woman is saying as we enter. I can't remember if she's Asher's mother or Micah's, but there's a pleasant twinkle in her eye that makes me like her.

"Visitors?" That's Damaris. She's enthroned in an armchair and hesitates a moment before getting up. "What a surprise."

Asher stands and steps forward as Cam goes to perch on Micah's knee, ignoring the expanse of space beside him on the couch. "Grandmother, you remember Zoe and Ronan. Take a seat, you two." It's not quite an order, but I step on Zoe's foot to stop her from making a smart-ass comment and drag her over to sit beside Micah. Garrett, in another armchair with Zac sitting on the arm, gives me a thumbs-up.

Zac's face is tense, and I wish he was closer so I could pet him.

"Asher, what's going on?" one of the men demands. I'm certain it's Asher's father.

"We have exciting news," Asher says, but his face doesn't match the words. His eyes are on his grandmother. "Micah, Zac, and I are forming a company to build a ski resort behind the village. Our research has shown it will be a wonderful tourist attraction for members of the community who want somewhere they can feel safe from human eyes. Garrett believes that when people see what an amazing haven we have up here, and once regular commuter travel is possible, it will lead to an influx of new residents."

"That sounds wonderful," the other mother says. I

know it's not Zac's mother—she's definitely Damaris's daughter. "But I thought those plans were considered years ago and turned out not to be feasible."

"The original concept was for a different location, Mom," Micah replies. "On top of that, with no way for tourists to get here during most of the ski season, there was no point in building a resort. That's changing now, thanks to the elves Garrett's hiring for the village."

"It sounds to me like this calls for a toast," one of the dads announces. "Let's celebrate this exciting new venture."

"No." Damaris's word cuts like a knife. Half of the room's occupants draw back in confusion, but the rest of us lean in for the fight. This is why we're here.

"We're not asking your permission, Grandmother," Asher says. It was agreed that as the oldest cousin present, he'd be the spokesman. "We don't need it. The investment will be from our personal funds. We'll apply to the village council to purchase the necessary land, and all relevant plans and permits will be obtained by us. This will bring jobs and visitors to the village—why would anyone vote against it?"

Her face darkens at his mocking tone. "Remember who you're speaking to, Asher Bailey. The council will look to me for my opinion, and I will *not* vote in favor of this."

"Why not?"

CHAPTER TWENTY-TWO

Zac

ASHER'S QUESTION hangs in the air. His and Micah's parents are frowning, and even my mom is looking at Grandmother with a tiny line between her brows.

"This idea of Zac's is foolish nonsense. You all need to focus on your duties and not on chasing empty dreams. The expense of this kind of undertaking—"

"The expense is ours, not anyone else's," Asher interrupts. His mother gasps softly. I can't remember the last time someone interrupted Grandmother. "And I resent your implication that we aren't focused. When have we ever failed to fulfil a duty?" He doesn't pause for her to answer. "This idea isn't foolish nonsense, which you'd know if you'd even listened to Zac when he brought it to you. Half an hour of your time is all he asked for, Grandmother, after decades of devotion to every duty you've ever volunteered him for. Why was that too much to ask?"

Grandmother's face transforms with fury. "Are you suggesting I don't love my family? Everything I do is for the good of this family and our people."

Asher nods. "I agree. I just don't think your definition of 'good' is always the same as ours."

The little puddle of silence is uncomfortable. Uncle Hal breaks it. "This seems to be family business. Perhaps our visitors—"

"They stay," I insist. "They're part of this."

Mom raises a brow at me, but I avoid her gaze. I know she loves me—that's not in doubt—but I honestly don't know whose side she's going to come down on, and that's a terrifying thought.

"Very well, Asher. Perhaps you'd like to expand on your little diatribe." Grandmother settles back in her chair and folds her arms.

Asher cocks his head. "You don't get it, do you? Even now, you're giving me *permission* to tell you what I think. I'm an adult, Grandmother, and you don't own me. I don't need your permission to speak. We've spent a long time jumping in whatever direction you told us to because we knew your intentions were good. None of us doubt that. But somewhere along the way, you've forgotten that we get to control our own lives."

She scoffs, but he continues.

"Your asinine matchmaking plans are a good example. Garrett and I weren't secretly dating. We met by coincidence two days before he came here. But your insistence on matchmaking was so abhorrent to me that I made up a boyfriend and borrowed a physical description for him from a man I never thought I'd see again."

Grandmother's expression doesn't change, but Asher's mom says, "What?"

"I talked Garrett into pretending we were in love. Our marriage was supposed to be one of convenience only—we have a legal document laying out the terms."

Now Grandmother's face pales as the extremes of the situation sink in.

Asher shrugs. "It all worked out, because Garrett and I actually did fall in love with each other. But do you see how little control you're willing to let us keep over our own lives? You didn't listen when I said I didn't want to be set up. No matter how many times or how loudly I protested. You. Didn't. Listen. And then you hatched up that ridiculous idea to match Cam and Zac together."

Ronan's jaw drops. Oops. He leans behind Zoe and nudges Cam, hissing, "What?"

"I'll tell you later," Cam whispers back.

"You're so sure you know what's best for us that you don't ask what we want. And when Zac came to you with something he wanted that would also benefit all of us, you wouldn't even hear him out. We're people, Grandmother. We're your family. You don't get to treat us like you own us."

Grandmother slowly stands, and I brace myself. Has she heard what Asher's been saying? Is this our chance to bring her on board?

"You deliberately deceived your family and married a stranger," she begins, and my disappointment is so strong, I almost choke on it.

Asher throws up his hands and turns away, defeat written all over his face. "I'm sorry," he tells me, and I nod. I was the one who insisted on this meeting first. Asher and Micah were all for letting Ronan threaten Grandmother from the outset.

"Grandmother." I cut her off before she can say anything else, standing and walking forward to look her in the eye. "We're taking our proposal to the village council and bidding for the land. The plan is a sound one. There's no reason why it should be refused."

"They'll refuse it because I'll tell them to," she declares, and even I have to admit defeat. I shake my head and wait for Ronan to speak up.

"No."

The word comes from an unexpected direction, and by the time I clue in that it's Mom who said it, she's already come to stand beside me.

"Dalia?" Grandmother's question is a warning.

"No, you will not tell them to refuse it. You'll look over the plans, and if they're as sound as the boys say, you'll vote in favor."

I've heard my mother use that tone before—she learned it at her mother's knee—but never when speaking to Grandmother. For as long as I can remember, they've always been on the same side.

"You didn't even listen?" she asks now. "My son—your grandson—came to you, and you wouldn't listen to him?" She shakes her head. "Asher was right. None of us have ever questioned your devotion, but that needs to go both ways. You need to recognize that we can make decisions for the good of the family too, without your interference." Putting her arm around my shoulders, Mom adds, "Zac has been a credit to us all. I'm certain he could get a job anywhere in the world with his skills, and yet he stays here to look after the village."

"They'd probably pay him anywhere else in the world, too," Ronan says quietly.

Mom's arm tightens. "What?"

Part of me wishes he hadn't brought that up—we've tossed enough baggage around for one night—but it also warms me that he's standing up for me. "He means I don't get paid for my work here. None of us do."

"That's ridiculous," Uncle Sol says, he and Uncle Hal

standing and coming forward. "How can you not get paid? You work full-time for the village."

"More than full-time," Micah offers helpfully. "I looked it up once, and Zac's doing the job of three people. But he doesn't work for the village. He's a volunteer."

Mom turns me to face her. "You're not on the village payroll?"

"Mother, how could this have happened?" Uncle Hal demands.

"Zac has enough money to support himself lavishly for the rest of his life," Grandmother says stubbornly.

"So does the village," Asher points out. "I would know, since I invest it. There's plenty of room in the payroll for Zac to have a wage and staff."

She glares at him.

"We're getting off-topic," Garrett interrupts. "While I agree that this is important and needs to be addressed—for Asher and Micah as well as Zac—the reason we're here tonight is to discuss the ski resort."

Grandmother's adamant, though. "I will not support it."

"Why not?" Uncle Sol sounds bewildered. "Why won't you even look at the idea?"

"Because Zac needs to stop with foolish dreams and stay focused on the duties he has!" Her shout is like a slap, and my aunts look anxiously toward the doorway, no doubt worried the kids heard.

I huff. "Denying me the things I want isn't going to keep me focused, Grandmother. Until now, that's been my family. And yeah, my duty. But I could train someone to take over those duties easily and go find another place where I can do more. Where I'm allowed to explore new things that interest and excite me. Where my contributions are heard and valued."

Mom's face turns to stone, and she stares down Grandmother. "You will support the plan."

"I will not."

"Yes, you will." That's Ronan. We all turn toward him. He hasn't moved from his position on the couch, back straight, hands in his lap. His face is absolutely calm, unlike Zoe's beside him.

"This is not your business," Grandmother says.

"It very much is. Support the plan, Damaris. I care more about the people who want this resort than I do about you... or your reputation."

Her eyes narrow as she understands his meaning. "Are you blackmailing me? You have no idea who you're dealing with, child."

Ronan laughs. "I know exactly who I'm dealing with. I know exactly what you're capable of. Do you know who my brother is? Do you think he let me come here without a full background report on you and your council? It's you who has no idea. You call me a child? I lived with monsters beyond your imagining for *thousands* of years. They raised me. I did things that make me want to die of shame now. *You* don't frighten me. Zac wants this resort, and it will be good for the village. You'll support it, or I'll destroy you." He leans forward, making sure she can see how serious he is. "And I won't regret it for a second."

I'm certain it's wrong—on many levels—for me to be so aroused by my almost-boyfriend threatening my grandmother. But Ronan fighting for me is the second-sexiest thing I've ever seen, the first being his kiss-swollen lips and passion-glazed eyes while we were fooling around on the couch today.

The face-off lasts for endless moments more, and then finally Grandmother gives a curt nod and turns away.

※

LATER, after stilted goodbyes and promises to our parents that we'll make time to talk, after I took Ronan home, cried on his shoulder for the lack of care my grandmother showed me, and then kissed him senseless for an hour… when I'm finally in my bedroom with the door closed, I pull out my phone and make a call.

"What?" Gideon growls.

"Love you too, Murder Baby," I manage, but it's lacking the usual teasing note, and he picks that up right away.

"What's happened?" The growl is gone, replaced by the deadly operative ready to race to our rescue.

I sigh. "We're fine," I assure him. "We… I guess we should have called you before we did this. Joseph and Anna too," I say in reference to his brother and sister.

"Tell me or I'm coming there to choke it out of you."

So I do. I tell him all of it…well, most. Some he knows —he's grumbled a few times about us not getting paid and the way Grandmother volunteers us for tasks. And I know Micah and Asher talked to him about my mood when he was here a few weeks back. I leave out what Grandmother did in the cave, just saying that Ronan threatened her. But he listens to the rest without interrupting, and then is silent.

"Are you mad? We shouldn't have ganged up on her." I cringe. Gideon's always been Grandmother's favorite, and he adores her.

"It was past time it happened," he surprises me by saying. "I should have pushed you to do it before now, but every time I visit, there's something else going on to distract me."

"Really? You… think we did the right thing?"

"Yes. Zac, why do you think my parents and my siblings and I don't live in Hortplatz?"

I shrug, even though he can't see me. "Why would you? You didn't live at the old settlement either. You did, but then you left."

"Exactly. Joseph and I left as soon as we were old enough. My parents stayed until Anna was old enough, and then they left too. Because we know exactly what Grandmother's like, and none of us are as self-sacrificing as the rest of you."

I gape like a gutted fish. "You work for CSG. Your whole life is about the community of species!"

"But I make those choices for myself. If I lived in Hortplatz and had grandmother interfering every time she had a whim, the family would have been torn apart a long time ago." It's his turn to sigh. "I should have protected you better when I saw what she was doing."

"Fuck you, I'm an adult. I can protect myself. And you, since you're the baby here!"

He snorts, which, for Gideon, is a sign of hysterical amusement. "So, Ronan Draco, huh? I wouldn't have picked that."

I hesitate. This is the real reason I called. "That's right. I forgot you know him."

"Fuck, Zac, you suck at this."

"What?" My indignance is not fake. I *do not* suck at this.

"If there's something you want to know, just ask. I don't have all day to talk about the guy you're fucking."

I don't bother to tell him there's been no fucking. It's not his business. I'm happy to take things as slow as Ronan needs—what's between us is more than just a hookup. "It's nothing, really. I shouldn't even be asking. I'm not sure if I want to know."

"I'm hanging up," he threatens.

"He said… He said some things about his childhood. And that he couldn't say more. It seemed painful for him, so I didn't want to push. But it's been stuck in my head all day, the way he said 'I can't talk about it.' And I started thinking… did he mean he can't, as in he signed an NDA or something?"

Gideon's silence is terrifying. "Are you asking me to look into his background?" he asks finally.

"No." The answer tumbles from me before I even form the thought. "No, he trusts me. I'm sorry. I shouldn't have brought it up."

"Zac." He pauses. "I barely know Ronan. I know Steffen a little more, but Ronan's practically a stranger to me, and I'm not going to lie: I never wanted to change that. When I met him, I didn't like him. That said, Ronan's childhood—both those twins'—was fucked-up. The man who raised them, he was… Let's just say he didn't give a shit about them or anyone else. When Ronan says he can't tell you, he didn't just sign an NDA. This is classified in two governments at the highest level. I shouldn't even be telling you this much. He *cannot* talk about it, not ever, not to anyone who doesn't already know. But he's been through the kind of shit that nobody should ever have to go through. So if you can't cope with not knowing, then walk away now before you hurt him even more. Because even though I don't like him, he doesn't deserve that."

Fuck. My breath feels frozen in my lungs, but I suck in enough oxygen to say, "Tell me one thing. Is he safe from it all now?"

"Yes. Those involved are dead."

"Then you and I never discussed this."

"Good. Now I'm going to pull my boyfriend away from work so we can spend a damn hour together on what's supposed to be our day off."

"Okay. Hey, Gideon?"

"What?"

"You didn't like the old Ronan, but I think you'll like the real Ronan." I can't hold back my smirk as I add, "He looked Grandmother right in the eye and told her he'd destroy her for my sake."

He snorts again. "You might be right. Wish I'd seen that." The line goes dead.

I toss my phone on the bed and exhale deeply. Annoyed, grumpy Gideon, I'm used to. The Gideon I just spoke to? That's not my cousin. That's the CSG agent who's considered one of the most elite and deadly operatives in the world. Whatever Ronan's life was before, he wants to be free of it now; wants to be his real self. And I'll do whatever he needs for that to happen.

CHAPTER TWENTY-THREE

Ronan

I'VE NEVER BEEN this happy before. It's uncanny. If someone had asked me in the past if I was happy, I would have said yes. Of course. But now that I'm actually happy, I know that wasn't true. Because these past five weeks have been so wonderful, I'm half afraid I've dreamed it all.

It helps that I love the work I'm doing. Now that I no longer feel like an imposter and have accepted that I'm still a dragon, even though my culture was stolen from me, I can see what I'm doing with new eyes. I still want to know everything about every piece I discover and catalogue, but now it's because *I* want to know, not because I need to prove something.

It's made work so much more fun, especially because the more knowledgeable I get, the more exciting each new find is. I decided to stop just reading notes and reports and to start actively asking questions, and now I'm connected with a network of experts across the world who are excited about this project and happy to talk about it. Some of them might even become friends, eventually. Fabian keeps texting to tell me how proud of me he is.

I'm proud of me too. Aside from working on something that's changing the modern perception of this world and its history, I'm helping to build a future for this village. I'm becoming part of the community and making friends and putting down roots. Because this is where I'm going to stay.

Things with Zac are new, and maybe they won't work out, but this is still going to be home for me, this place where people now smile when they see me and call out greetings and ask if I'm coming to karaoke or trivia night or if I'll be on their team for the snowball fight. Where Arne at the pub remembers my preferred drink, and Griff at the grocery store offered to order me specialty baking supplies from a wholesaler as long as I don't open a bakery to compete with Greta. Greta, on the other hand, turned up on my doorstep one evening to say she'd heard about my pastries, and was I interested in making some occasional money on the side? We now have an agreement that when she gets a big special order or has an event to bake for, I'll help out. She also hinted that when my work cataloguing the vault is done and we start seeing an influx of visitors, there might be a more regular job for me. Garrett pouted for an hour when he heard, then told me he was working on a "competitive offer" to keep me at the museum.

And then there's Zac. He's filled my every spare minute this past month, and I don't want it any other way. Just having him *there*, lying on the kitchen sofa reading a journal, or watching TV in the living room while I experiment with baking something new, is so comfortable and amazing. He's my most eager taste-tester, and when I over-kneaded the scones because I was distracted and they turned out hard as rocks, he teased me out of my sulk, then went and got some resin so we could turn them into something useful. I now have scone bookends, paperweights, and, my personal favorite, the scone pyramid doorstop.

He took me camping in the snow, and we lay under the stars for hours, just staring up at the constellations and talking in soft murmurs about little things. Then we burrowed into our snow cave and slept tangled together in our own cozy little world.

I took him flying. We left in the stillness of predawn, dragging Zoe out of bed to help with the harness, then watched the sun rise as we banked over a glacier. With his directions, we saw some of the most beautiful, remote places in the Alps, just the two of us.

And when we got back to Hortplatz, just before lunch, there was a crowd assembled to watch us land. I stayed in dragon form and let the children swarm me under Zac's watchful eye while Zoe and Micah took care of the harness.

Garrett tells me that I'm now the official school mascot, and I took a day off from working in the cave to go to the school and talk about being a dragon. Isaac, Micah's little brother, widened his big brown eyes at me and asked if I could please shift for them again, and that's how I spent an hour one afternoon in my dragon form with a dozen or so children strewn over me, napping and talking quietly about all the adventures they plan to go on. It was… humbling. It made me sad that for all the luxury of my own childhood, I never had that sense of absolute security and freedom. But knowing I can be part of that for other children, maybe even children of my own one day… that's enough to soothe any of my old scars. I talked about it with Steffen that night, and he understood.

We're closer now, he and I. He told me he ran a background check on Zac and approves of him as my boyfriend, and I yelled at him about prying into my life without permission, even though I love that he wants to. I love it even more that I knew I could yell at him and he'd still be there for me.

So… I'm happy. I have friends, here and elsewhere. I have hobbies and work I love.

I have Zac. Quiet moments alone, talking or watching TV. Time together with friends. Hot, impassioned kissing, our hands sliding all over each other, building the burning need between us, teasing something more.

I think I'm ready for the more.

Zac's been amazing. Patient. Caring. Always there for me. Ready to give me anything I want. He's never indicated in any way that going slow is a problem, even though I can literally feel the evidence that he wants more. He won't ask for it. He'll wait for me to make that move.

The problem is… I'm not sure how. I'm not even completely sure how… *it* all works.

I know the mechanics, of course. I've read books, watched porn. But I'm pretty sure there are bits that get left out for artistic purposes. And even if I had a detailed how-to manual, I know from learning to fly and bake that sometimes, the first attempt doesn't work. It can be awkward or uncomfortable or hard as a rock.

I think this analogy got off-track. Hard as a rock is probably a good thing when it comes to sex.

But I don't want to make our first time together bad for him because it's my first time ever and I don't know what I'm doing. And it's not like I can have my first time with someone else to get the practice in—not that I'd even want to. Just the thought of being with someone other than Zac is blech.

Which means I need to ask for help.

Now's the best time. Zac left twenty minutes ago, still excited because today we finally got a completely snow-cleared patch in the village. I'm told that won't last, but it's a big sign that spring has come to Hortplatz, and it made Zac adorably giddy.

I pull out my phone and open the Ro Ro Ro The Group thread. Lately it's been more about cat memes and videos of people being idiots than actual advice, which I love.

> Need help. You're not allowed to laugh.

It takes less than thirty seconds for multiple people to start typing.

HAGEN:

> Can't guarantee that, but I promise you'll never know

FABIAN:

> Are you in trouble? If you're naked and tied to furniture, don't worry. Your joints are more flexible than you realize.

SOPHIE:

> You can tell me anything. I'm a healer. I've seen it all.

SOPHIE:

> But if the pus is orange, don't touch it

DUSTIN:

> Can I come visit soon? I want more cookies. The ones you sent got eaten so fast.

I take a second to wonder what would make pus orange, then decide to ignore all their comments and just push on.

I never said anything because it's private, but I've never had sex before

There's a moment where none of them type. It's like they don't know what to say. People who've met them would be shocked.

FABIAN:

Um. I'm sorry, but I don't get it?

HAGEN:

Do you mean with a demon? Are you and Zac not... Okay. That's cool. It's just like with all the other species. You'll be fine!

No. I've never had sex

DUSTIN:

With a man? I never asked, are you bi? Pan?

This is excruciating. If I didn't need their help so much, I'd just give up.

SOPHIE:

You're all idiots. Ronan, are you asexual?

Thank fuck, something I can actually answer.

No. I want to have sex. I just never have.

FABIAN:

I still don't get it. Not ever?

SOPHIE:

Some people don't, Fabian. That's valid.

FABIAN:

> No, I get that. I know what ace is and I respect it. If you don't want it, you don't want it. Everyone needs to have fun for sex to be good, right? But Ronan says he wants it.

SOPHIE:

> All our lives take different paths. We don't all make the same choices or have the same opportunities. It's not important that Ronan didn't have sex before. What matters is that he wants to now and is ASKING FOR OUR HELP

For the first time, the reminder that other people know about my past—who I was, what I did—doesn't make me flinch. Instead, I answer Dustin's question.

> I'm gay. I've only ever been attracted to men. And porn with women doesn't do much for me unless I'm focused on the guy.

HAGEN:

> Is Zac pressuring you for sex?

I laugh out loud.

> No. Zac's amazing. I said I wanted to go slow and he's never pushed for more. That's part of the problem now. I don't know how to show him I'm ready.

FABIAN:

> That's easy. Strip naked and say 'wanna fuck?'

DUSTIN:

> Or just strip naked. That usually does it for me. Sometimes I pretend to be reading too. That drives Rob WILD

I'm sure they're right about that. And okay, I can do that. I know Zac wants me—I have no fear of rejection.

> But then what? I want it to be good for him. I don't want to be some stupid virgin who knows nothing and he has to do all the work. I'm not even sure if I want to top or bottom.

SOPHIE:

> This is outside my field of expertise, so I'm going to let the others handle it. But, from a medical perspective, you know the lube spell, right? If you don't, make sure one of these fools teaches you.

The lube spell? That sounds like it could be useful.

> Thanks, Sophie. Do we need to use condoms? I haven't seen any here, but all the porn I've watched has them.

HAGEN:

> Sounds like you've been watching human porn. They're the only species that can pass diseases that way. You and Zac won't need them.

FABIAN:

> But if you've only watched human porn, do you know about the dick thing?

Dick thing?

> I know human dicks are different from ours.

DUSTIN:

> All the species have different dicks. Demons are the most like humans, though. Just... bigger. And less... shapely.

HAGEN:

More like a Coke can. But not exactly. You'll love it.

FABIAN:

You REALLY will. Trust me. But you said you don't know if you want to top or bottom?

How can I know without trying? And halfway through sex is probably a bad time to discover I hate the position we're in and he loves it.

DUSTIN:

Those are two different issues. The first one, we can help with. The second is all on you. You have to talk to him about what you both prefer BEFORE you get too far.

But I don't know what I prefer!

HAGEN:

Like Dustin said, we can help. What's the address of the PO Box where the town's mail goes? I'm sending you some stuff.

I give him the address, then add,

What kind of stuff?

HAGEN:

The kind that will help you figure out if you're a top or a bottom. They'll be there in three or four days.

FABIAN:

> Meanwhile, I just emailed you a subscription to a really good community porn site. Don't worry, I have a pile of guest memberships that are about to expire. When you set up your profile, let me know what it is so I can add you as a friend and you can see some of my bookmarked videos.

I purse my lips. After everything I've heard, I'm not sure I want to see porn that Fabian's bookmarked.

DUSTIN:

> Trust us. Watch the porn and play around with yourself. Not just your dick—your ass too. I'm going to send you the lube spell. It's super easy. Use plenty the first time you finger yourself, and just relax. You'll work out what you like.

HAGEN:

> If Zac's as amazing as you say he is, he'll understand that you're not a sexpert your first time

> I just want it to be good for us both.

DUSTIN:

> Does he know you're a virgin? That's kind of important.

> I told him I don't have a lot of experience and want to take things slow.

FABIAN:

> Dude. No. Consent means everyone gets to know the facts. You don't need to make it a big deal, but you should tell him it's your first time.

DUSTIN:

> Yep. Tell him you THINK you're a
> top/bottom/versatile—whatever you work
> out—but that sex with someone else is a
> new experience for you.

HAGEN:

> Some guys dig the whole virgin thing. He's
> been good with waiting, so he'll probably
> think it's special that you've never been
> with anyone else.

I get the distinct feeling that in Zac's shoes, Hagen would run so fast in the other direction, he'd be a blur.

FABIAN:

> The most important thing to remember is
> that it's okay for either of you to say no or
> stop or slow down. Sometimes things are
> going great but then one thing just feels off.
> Don't think you gotta keep going. Talk to
> Zac and listen when he talks to you.

I really didn't expect so much of this advice to be centered on feelings and consent. It casts my friends in a new light.

FABIAN:

> And may you both come like Niagara Falls!

Okay, that's more like it.

DUSTIN:

> Take your time exploring things over the
> next few days. Make sure you're ready and
> feel confident and know where to find the
> prostate. It's in the same spot for all
> species.

HAGEN:

And let me know if you have questions when the package arrives. Some of the instructions aren't that great.

Instructions? What the fuck is he sending me?

CHAPTER TWENTY-FOUR

Zac

I PACE AGITATEDLY along the upstairs hallway. I was pacing in my bedroom, but there wasn't enough room to get a good stride going. How can a man think when he constantly has to stop and turn? And I need to think. I need to understand how, after a month of being the happiest I've ever been, of having everything in my life fall into place as if by magic, I could somehow have fucked it up.

What did I do? That's what I can't work out. It was all going so well. Grandmother's still pissed, but we expected that. She loves us, and eventually she'll come around. In the meantime, our parents called us over to Uncle Hal and Aunt Hilda's house the day after the big confrontation to apologize for not understanding exactly what was going on and not protecting us better. We're grown adults, but there was something about having my mom say she wished she'd looked out for me more that made me feel validated. She and I have talked about personal stuff a few times since, and even though I would've said we've always been close, it's different now. I like it better this way. I told her I'm falling in love with Ronan, and she's made it a mission to get to know him better. I don't think he ever really had a mother figure—he's mentioned a nurse when he was small, but never anyone who cuddled him—and even though I know my mom can be scary to a lot of people, he seems to see beyond that to the mom part of her. They get along like a house on fire, and I love it.

Asher filed the papers for the legal incorporation of our new company, and the village council, with Grandmother's grudging approval, has agreed to sell us the land for the resort. Micah and I have been working on the plans, with a lot of input from Zoe, who's spent more time in ski resorts than any of us, and, surprisingly, Aunt Cami. She's really excited about the idea of a family-friendly community vacation destination. Unbeknownst to us, she's a member of a lot of online community parenting forums, and she says the lack of safe places for community children to just be themselves while on vacation is something that comes up a lot. She's convinced that with the right advertising, we can be fully booked for a whole season before we even officially open. Zoe just smiled smugly and said, "See?"

And Ronan… Ronan is amazing. He's the piece of my life I didn't even know was missing. I know he's still coming to terms with a lot of stuff about himself and his past and his relationship with his brother, especially, but seeing him slowly gain his confidence and be the person he wants to be is the most beautiful thing I've ever witnessed.

He's not shy about showing affection, either. At first I thought he would be, because that initial kiss was so reticent, but now that he's sure of what he's doing, he doesn't hesitate to touch me or steal kisses wherever and whenever he wants to. He's not clingy, but he likes for us to be in contact—holding hands in public, snuggled together on the couch, legs touching while we eat. We're almost always connected, and I love it. Sure, I'm being eaten alive with sexual frustration and have never jerked off this much in my life, not even when I was a teenager and just discovering the joy of it. But he wants to go slow, and I don't want to do anything that might fuck things up between us.

Except somehow, I have.

This past week, he's been different. It started at the end of last week, although I didn't notice right away. He's been… not distant. When we're together, doing things, out and about, everything's fine. It's all the same. But when we're at his place, just hanging out, the night winding down, he… It's like he's waiting for me to leave. He's still into everything we do, eager even, but before when I finally made a move to go, he'd be pouty and ask for just a few more minutes or one more kiss. Now… now he lets me go. It's like he's losing interest, or not as invested, and I don't get it. Nothing's changed for me except that I want him more than ever. I'm within inches of losing my heart to him completely, and it seems like he's just okay with me.

I must have done something. I just don't know what.

Asher's bedroom door flies open, and Garrett's tousled head pokes out, an annoyed expression on his face. "Whatever the fuck crawled up your ass, can you pace somewhere else? Some of us are trying to sleep. It's a work night. I have to deal with children in the morning, Zac. *Children.* Do you know how much energy children have? I need *rest,* not you thumping back and forth like an elephant." His head disappears, the door slams, and I cringe.

Note to self: Garrett gets grumpy when his sleep's disturbed.

I'm not achieving anything here, anyway. I can't think of what I might've done to have caused this change in Ronan. Maybe he's talked about it with his friends? I eye

Asher's door. Ronan and Garrett have gotten pretty close. I could ask… but not right now. Garrett's unlikely to be receptive to questions at this precise moment.

Maybe one of Ronan's other friends would be?

I tiptoe into my room, close the door, and grab my phone. I know I have her number…

> Hey, are you still up?

It's an agonizingly long two minutes before her answer pops up.

ZOE:

> Yeah. Everything okay?

I don't bother to text, just call her.

"Zac? What's wrong?"

"It's Ronan," I blurt, and she gasps.

"Is he injured? Where are you? I'm on my way!"

Fuck.

"No, Zoe, he's fine. I'm sorry, I didn't mean to scare you. He's fine."

Her shaky breath makes me feel like the worst kind of scum. "You're an asshole and I hate you," she says finally, but there's no heat in it. "Why are you calling, then?"

I hesitate. She's Ronan's friend—would she really tell me if he was losing interest in me?

"Zac," she warns.

"Has Ronan said anything about me? About… about not wanting to be with me?"

Her laugh is ridiculously reassuring. "Are you high or something? Taken a paranoid pill?"

"So that's a no, then."

"Of course it's a fucking no. Did you seriously call me

this late to ask such a stupid question? Ronan's batshit crazy in love with you. Any idiot can see that."

Doubt sets in. Could I be imagining it? Maybe I'm just overreacting?

Then I remember the almost cheerful way he stood up tonight when I said I had to go, the way he gave me an almost perfunctory kiss and then stood back with an expression of "off you go." It's such a far cry from the way he clung to me for "one more kiss" last week that I can't dismiss it.

"There's more to this than just insecurity, isn't there?" Zoe huffs in resignation. "Tell me what you're thinking."

I do, feeling stupid the whole time. I like Zoe, but she's closer to Ronan than to me. This isn't the kind of conversation we'd normally have. I don't know who else to talk about this with who might actually have some insight, though, so I swallow my pride and bare my soul.

She takes her time to process it all. "I really want to say you're overreacting," she says finally. "Like… he could be preoccupied with something. When's your birthday? Maybe he's planning a gift."

"January."

"Probably not that, then. Look… you know I'm his friend first, right? I mean I know you and I were friends first, but he's—"

"No, I get it," I assure her. "I'm glad. He needs friends that put him first. I'm not asking you to spill secrets, I swear. I just want to know what I fucked up so I can fix it."

"It's a good thing you're not asking me to spill secrets because I wouldn't. I'll talk to him, see if there's something going on. *If* there is, I'll encourage him to talk to you about it. But I'm not going to go behind his back to tell you anything. Whatever it is, either he'll talk to you, or you'll have to find another way to figure it out."

It's not perfect, not the answers I was hoping for, but it's better than nothing. "Thank you, Zoe. I'm grateful. He… It really felt like things were working out for us, you know? He loves being here now, and he's talking about working part-time at the museum as a guide and part-time for Greta baking, and I thought all the roots he was putting down meant he wanted to stay here with me. But maybe he just wants to stay here, and I'm not in the equation."

"Aren't you supposed to be the level-headed cousin?"

She hangs up before I can reply.

I stretch out on my bed, thinking. I still don't have answers, but I have a lead… kind of. In the meantime, something Zoe said tweaked my brain. I scroll through my contacts and hit another number.

"I wish I had never given any of you my number," he answers, and I grin.

"Hello to you too, Murder Baby. Having a bad day at work?"

Gideon grunts. "It was fine until you called. What do you want now? Did you set Grandmother's house on fire?"

I blink. "Did we— No! What the fuck, Gideon? Why would you even ask that?"

"Why. Are. You. Calling. Me?"

I give up. He has no patience. "I need you to ask Ronan's brother when their birthday is."

The line goes so silent that I pull the phone away from my ear, wondering if the call dropped out. It hasn't.

"Hello? Gideon? Can you hear me?"

"Unfortunately. You want me to what?"

"I need to know when Ronan's birthday is so I can make sure it's celebrated properly. And I can't ask him— you said yourself his childhood was fucked-up. I don't want to trigger anything." I hesitate. "Could you ask Steffen about that too? If a birthday party and gifts would be painful for Ronan?"

"Fuck my fucking life," he mutters. "Let me make sure I understand this. You want me, in the middle of my workday, to leave my office and go to the office of another government to ask *Steffen Draco*, the most paranoid being alive, when his *birthday* is? Information that could hypothetically be used to steal his identity?"

I hear someone in the background say, "What?" but I ignore it in my hurry to remind him, "And ask if a party would trigger Ronan. Don't forget that."

The cursing that fills my ear is impressive but a waste of time. He could be halfway there by now. Still, knowing Gideon as I do, the best option is to wait him out. He gets cranky if you interrupt him.

He's mid-word when his voice fades and someone else says, "Hello? Who's this?"

I wince, recognizing the voice. "Zac. Gideon's cousin. Is that Alistair?" I met Garrett's cousin for the first time at Asher's wedding. It was… memorable. I've seen him a few times since, mainly to do with the cave and vault, but also when Cam was kidnapped. He was like a completely different person that day.

"Yep! What's this about Steffen's birthday?" His ridiculously cheerful demeanor is… daunting.

"Uh, it's actually Ronan's birthday I'm interested in. We're dating. But I don't want to ask him, and since he and Steffen are twins—"

"Say no more. I'm in! Surprise parties for the win, am I right? Don't worry, I've got you covered."

"You… do?" Why am I suddenly worried?

"Sure. We're family now. Cousin-in-law of my cousin, and all that. I'll talk to my bros, and we'll get the details on when Ronan's birthday is."

"And..." Shit, does Alistair know as much as Gideon? How much can I say? I'm not supposed to know any of it. "Some people don't like surprises, and I get the feeling Ronan's childhood wasn't always great. So could you find out if he's okay with birthday parties?"

Alistair makes a humming sound. "That one's gonna be trickier. Might actually have to talk to Steffen. But don't worry, I'll get what you need. Give me your number."

I do, wondering if it's a mistake.

"Leave it with me. This is going to be fun."

CHAPTER TWENTY-FIVE

Ronan

I stroll into my kitchen, smile as I pat my gorgeous stand mixer that Zac bought me, and open the pantry. What should I bake on this glorious Saturday morning? Zac's coming over later, and I want to surprise him with something delicious. Hmm… cheese Danish, maybe? Or I saw a recipe for a cheesy choux bread that looked very easy —I could get something complicated and sweet started, then do that for a savory too.

My phone chimes with the tone for Ro Ro Ro The Group, and I fish it out of my pocket.

HAGEN:

Ro, I gotta ask you some questions and you can't ask why. It's bro code.

Bro code? I don't know what that is, but it sounds important. I can respect bro code.

Sure

SOPHIE:

Oh no. Ronan, you're supposed to reserve the right not to answer if it will incriminate you.

Bro code is starting to sound complicated.

Can't I just… not answer?

DUSTIN:

It doesn't work that way. But Hagen will make an exception because now we're all dying to know what the questions are.

HAGEN:

Do you like surprises?

Only the good ones.

Someone giving me a book of local recipes? Good surprise. Finding out the man who raised me was a megalomaniac who stole me and robbed me of my heritage while also torturing my twin? Not so much.

HAGEN:

That's supremely not helpful. When's your birthday?

I know what birthdays are. I'd never heard of them before coming to Earth, but the species here celebrate them, and apparently the elves and dragons were quick to get on board with that. Everyone loves an excuse for a party, presents, and cake.

But…

I don't know

There's a moment of no typing, and I cringe. Nope.

No. I'm not going to feel bad about this. New Ronan wouldn't.

HAGEN:

Shit. I just figured Steffen didn't tell anyone his because he's paranoid

Maybe that's true. But I honestly don't know mine. Would Brandt be able to tell? Or could I just pick a day?

I'm really curious to know why he's asking, but whatever bro code is, I'm not breaking it. Anyway, the more I think about it, the more I like the idea of having a birthday. Do I need to consult with Steffen about the day, since we're twins?

DUSTIN:

This can't be right. You've been with us for years. How have we not ever thrown a party for you?

FABIAN:

I'M SO SORRY! We're the worst. I assumed that because Stef doesn't want to celebrate his and won't even tell us when it is that you wouldn't either.

SOPHIE:

Steffen doesn't know. Brandt doesn't either. He was able to estimate approximately when, but not exactly.

I don't ask how she knows this. Sophie was the one who healed Steffen's wounds—and did a health check on me. She and Brandt—and Steffen—wanted to know if I knew anything about our mother or the circumstances of our birth. I don't. *He* told me little, and of what he did say, it's hard to know how much is true.

HAGEN:

Okay, so you don't have a birthday. Cool cool. Wanna pick one? Or not. Maybe you're not into the whole birthday thing.

Fuck that. I want a birthday with a huge party and a lot of people telling me how amazing I am just for being born. I wonder if Zac would help me plan one?

The birthday thing sounds perfect. Do Stef and I need to pick a day together? Because I don't think he'll be into it.

DUSTIN:

I'll pay to watch someone ask him to choose a birthday and let us throw him a party

SOPHIE:

Hard pass

FABIAN:

I'll do it! But someone has to protect me from him

HAGEN:

What if Ronan's birthday is just Ronan's? And if Steffen decides he wants one, he can pick it for himself. They're twins, not clones. Individuality is allowed.

SOPHIE:

Yes to individuality, but I don't think you understand how the birthday thing works with twins.

FABIAN:

I agree with Hagen. Ronan can pick his own birthday, and Stef can... Maybe we just don't tell him.

DUSTIN:

He's going to find out when we throw
Ronan a mega-awesome birthday party.

I'll talk to Stef about it. But I get to choose
my own birthday, and he has to find a way
to deal.

I'm proud of myself for typing that. Steffen and I are continuing to improve our relationship. He's putting in more effort now, and we talk every week. Sometimes Wil is there, too, and I can't believe I never picked up on their relationship before. I know they've gone out of their way to keep it secret, but the clues are all there for anyone who really wants to work it out. I love their dynamic, but it's also helped me to realize it's not what I want. A supportive partner who cares about my feelings? Yes, definitely. But I also want public affection. I *love* touching Zac, holding hands, having him drop a casual kiss on my cheek or hair when we're out in public. Knowing that someone is so openly willing to show their feelings for me is… empowering. And I get to do the same for him.

So while Steffen and I are twins and building closer ties, we don't have to be the same. I don't need him to agree with or approve of everything I do. I know now that he'll still want to be my brother even if I'm not exactly like him. And that means I can pick a birthday, and he can accept that, just like I'll accept that he might not want to pick one for himself.

HAGEN:

So… when's your birthday?

I take a moment to think about it.

May 2nd

I don't think anyone else will get it—well, maybe Steffen and Brandt. And Wil. That's the day I pretended to be Steffen to gain access to the DEA offices and tried to hack his computer. The day Wil caught me and I first met Brandt. The day that set me on the path to being free.

The day of my rebirth.

Those first few months were painful and difficult, both physically and emotionally. But I'm still here, and now I'm me.

DUSTIN:

> That's only two weeks away! It's going to be hard to plan the perfect party in that time. My circus contact needs at least three months' notice

HAGEN:

> May 2. Got it. Hold off on the party planning for now

FABIAN:

> Why? Ronan deserves a party, and we're his friends.

HAGEN:

> Bro code. Just do it.

SOPHIE:

> I'm not a bro. Why can't we plan a party?

The chat goes quiet for a minute, and I check the Wi-Fi connection.

SOPHIE:

> Let's hold off on the party planning for now. We can have a virtual celebration on the day and then a real party when you next visit.

What…? I start typing a question, but my doorbell rings, and according to my magic, it's Zoe.

I cram my phone back into my pocket and go let Zoe in. To my surprise, she's carrying a big box.

"This is yours," she says. "I picked it up for you at the post office. What's in it?"

"No idea." I take it and step back to let her inside while I check the label. That's my name, but the return address is just a delivery depot. "Oh, wait—Hagen said he was sending me something. It's taken longer than he thought, so I forgot about it."

We traipse into the kitchen. "No baking today?" she asks, unwinding her scarf and dumping it with her parka on one of the kitchen chairs.

"I haven't started yet. I got distracted by the group chat." Setting the box on the table, I go find the scissors to cut the tape. I could use magic, but where's the fun in that?

"Okay, listen, I need to talk to you about something, but first, you know I'm your bestie, right?"

I don't look up from slitting the tape at the sides of the box. "What? Of course."

"Good. Because I am. And I'm always on your side. But I also want what's best for you, which is why— What the fuck?"

The scissors drop from my hands to clatter to the floor as I stare into the box. "Oh no," I breathe. Everything inside is packaged, but the pictures on the packaging… and the names…

"What the hell is a Ding Dong Dildo?" Zoe reaches out to grab it, and I slap her hand away. "Ow! Ronan, I just wanted to look at it!"

"I…" My lips press together hard, but I can't help it. Laughter bursts from me.

"Care to let me in on the joke?" Zoe's taken advantage of my distraction to raid the box, and she's holding up a hot pink dildo in a clear, molded plastic package. "Ding Dong Dildo. Guaranteed to ring your bell," she reads. "A friend sent you this?"

Still chuckling, I sit down at the table and try to avoid looking into the box. "Remember how I told you I'm not that experienced with relationships and sex? Well, the truth is, I have zero. Zac and I have been taking things slow, but I'm ready for more, only…" I feel my cheeks getting hot. I guess I still find this embarrassing, even though I know I shouldn't. "The thing is, I didn't really know what I even wanted. What I like. And I want our first time together to be special, not with me being all fumbling and weird. So I asked my friends for advice."

Zoe winces. "Do I want to know how that went? Although"—she reaches into the box and pulls out a smaller box with World of Wangs blazoned on the lid—"I can probably make an educated guess."

I snort. "They were actually pretty helpful. They sent me some good interspecies porn and told me to play around with myself and see what… you know. And they said I should talk to Zac."

There's a strange look on Zoe's face. "Was this about a week ago?"

I nod. "Yeah."

She glances back at the big box. "And then one of them sent you a bunch of sex toys to experiment with. Including a Fleshlight, anal beads, and an assortment of vibrating cock rings." She turns over the smaller box in her hands and reads the description on the packaging. "And this is a collection of interspecies dildos. He forgot the lube, though. From the looks of some of these, you're definitely going to want lube."

Standing, I lean over the box. "There's a spell for that. Dustin sent it to me. It's super easy."

"Of course there is," she mutters. "I should have guessed."

I take the items she unpacked and put them back in the box, then push it to the other side of the table. "This is probably more than you were expecting this morning. You wanted to talk to me about something?"

She nods. "Yeah. But, um… just to be clear, this past week you've been, uh… experimenting with yourself? When Zac's not around, I mean. You've been taking time to… play. And… explore what you like?"

Do besties usually share this much? Does she want details? I'm not sure I'd be comfortable with that. But if I take the questions at face value, they're not so bad. "Yes."

Another nod, this time more thoughtful. "Okay. That's great. Your friends are right. You should talk to Zac. Soon. Today, even."

I make a face. "I know. Probably not today, though. He's coming over in a while, and I won't get a chance to play with all this stuff until he leaves tonight. But definitely soon. I can't wait for us to…" I trail off. "Well, you know."

"Yep. I do. So…" She stands. "I'm gonna let you put this stuff away and get on with your day. I'll see you later, though—karaoke at the pub tonight, remember?"

"Zac and I are looking forward to it. Well, I am," I amend. Zac goes because I ask him to.

She looks at me strangely again. "You know I love you, right? And I'd never do anything to hurt you? I want you to have what you want."

"Yeah, I know. Zoe, is everything okay?"

Her usual grin appears. "Oh yeah. Never better. I'll show myself out."

Before I can ask anything else, she sweeps up her stuff and hurries to the hallway. I hear the front door open and close seconds later. Did she even stop to put her parka on first?

I shake my head. Whatever's going on with her, she'll tell me when she's ready. Or I'll get it out of her tonight at karaoke.

CHAPTER TWENTY-SIX

Zac

In the two days since I spoke to Zoe, Ronan's said nothing about it. He's still the same loving, affectionate, *perfect* boyfriend, except when it comes to the end of the evening, he's eager to see me leave. Tonight, especially. I don't get it. He got a little tipsy during karaoke, couldn't keep his hands off me, was all over me when we got back to his place, so much so that I thought for sure things had changed. That they were back to normal.

But when, after an hour of hot, steamy kisses, I tested the waters by suggesting it might be time for me to go home, he actually leapt off the couch in his haste to send me on my way.

That was so not the outcome I'd been expecting.

As I leave the teleport room and head toward my bedroom, I wonder if maybe I need to be the one to talk to Ronan about this. I don't want him to think I'm pressuring him for more, but I also want him to know that if he *does* want to end things, that's… well, it's not okay, but he's allowed to do that.

"Zac? Is that you?"

I freeze and spin toward the living room. "Zoe?" What's she doing here this late?

She appears in the doorway. "Hi! Uh, I just need a few minutes of your time." Her smile is wide and... fake. My stomach drops.

Oh no. She talked to Ronan and she's here to give me bad news.

No, wait. She said she wouldn't do that.

But what if Ronan told her to?

Except Ronan wouldn't have been the way he was tonight if he was expecting Zoe to break up with me for him... would he?

No.

So why's Zoe here?

Standing here isn't going to get me answers. "Sure." I start toward her. "Uh, where are Asher and Garrett?"

"They went to bed. Asher tried to kick me out first, but I wouldn't go."

I nod like that makes perfect sense as she settles onto the couch. "Of course." Joining her, I raise an expectant brow. "What's up?"

"Ahhhh—"

The strident ringing of my phone cuts her off, and relief crosses her face. "You better answer that."

"No, it's..." I glance at the screen. Alistair. "Actually, if you don't mind?"

She gestures for me to go ahead, and I answer.

"Hi, Alistair."

"Cuz, I've totally got the goods."

Cuz? Oh fuck, has he adopted me?

"The... goods?"

"Ronan's birthday is soon, so you need to get things moving. Lucky for you, I am a party planner supreme, the king of soirees, the best-a at fiestas, so I can help."

I'm suddenly regretting all the life choices that led to this moment.

"I don't think—"

"That's cool; I can do the thinking. One thing first, though—I've been told we gotta make it clear that just because it's Ronan's birthday doesn't mean it's Steffen's."

There is literally no reply I can give right now that would make sense.

"Okay," I manage finally. What else am I supposed to say?

"I knew you'd get it. Hagen said you would."

Who… wait, Hagen, as in Ronan's friend from the chat?

"I wanted this kept a secret from Ronan!" My voice rises, but Alistair just scoffs.

"Please. This isn't my first epic surprise party. Hagen didn't give us away—bro code."

Talking to Alistair is going to give me a migraine.

"Just… When is his birthday?"

"May second."

Fuck, that's soon. I'm probably going to need help planning a party that quickly… but not Alistair's. My gaze goes to Zoe, who's staring at her lap, pretending not to listen.

"And he definitely wouldn't be traumatized or triggered by a party?" I ask, mostly to get a reaction out of her. Just like I hoped, her head snaps up, eyes wide.

"Dude, no. He's totally on board with the whole birthday thing. Hagen said go at it full force. But we gotta invite the dragons, okay? And it's gotta be a huge blowout."

"Got it." I can give Ronan a huge blowout party in two weeks. I'll get the whole village involved. They love him now… except maybe Grandmother, but she definitely respects him, and that's probably more important.

"So I was thinking—"

I cut him off. "Let me nail down a few details, and I'll call you back in a day or so to get things rolling. It's still pretty cold up here, so I need to make sure I can get an indoor space that will hold us all."

"Smart thinking. My pretty face does *not* look good with blue lips. But my glitter guy needs as much notice as possible, so don't delay."

His… glitter guy? He has a *glitter guy*? Do I want Ronan's birthday to be overtaken by glitter?

I remember his delight when Griff at the grocery store got him edible glitter to decorate cookies and cakes with, and resign myself to a glittery party.

"Tomorrow night," I promise. "Talk to Hagen again and tell him I might need some more inside info."

"On it. Laters." The call ends, and I stare at the phone for a long second. *Laters?* Hellhounds are fucking weird, and that one's the weirdest of them all.

"Zac?"

Ah. Zoe. I put my phone away and look at her. "I'm going to need your help planning a birthday party for Ronan on really short notice."

"I didn't know his birthday was coming up." She's frowning.

"Me neither. I had to sneak around behind his back to find out. But I've been assured that he'd be fine with a party, so I'm throwing him a party. A big one."

She nods. "Okay. Sure. That'll be fun."

"I'll get the planning started tomorrow, but… what was it you needed?"

Her eyes widen. "You need to go back to Ronan's."

"What?" My heart starts to pound. "Why? Is he okay? I just left there!"

"He's fine. Sorry. He's fine. Don't freak out. Just… go back there."

I rub my forehead. "Zoe, I just had to talk to Garrett's insane cousin. Don't you start being weird too. What's going on?"

She grabs my phone out of my hands and holds it behind her back. "Oh no, you left your phone at Ronan's. You'd better go get it. Don't want to miss any important calls."

She's officially lost it. Did we do this to her? Is living in Hortplatz really that hard? I thought she liked it here.

Her eyes are locked on my face, and I can tell she's trying to send me a message of some kind, but fucked if I know what it is. "Zoe—"

"Zac. Go. To. Ronan's. Now."

I'm not going to win this. "Fine. I'll go back to Ronan's. And when he asks why, I'll tell him you've lost your marbles." I hold out my hand. "Can I have my phone back now?"

She passes it over, and I teleport out the second it's in my hand.

The teleport room at Ronan's house is dark, because of course he isn't expecting me. I give my eyes a second to adjust, then head out into the hallway. It's dark too, and I assume Ronan's gone to be—

A moan echoes through the house.

I go on high alert. Is Ronan hurt? Did he fall? Is someone here?

The next moan is… confusing. I could swear he said my name. Maybe he hit his head and has a concussion? Or someone's hurt him and he's calling for me?

I slip along the hallway as quietly as I can. If there's

another person here, they don't need any warning before I rip them to shreds.

The door to Ronan's bedroom is open, and light is spilling into the hallway. As I creep closer to the doorway, Ronan cries out, "Zac!"

I leap forward, prepared to defend him. But there's nobody else there. Just Ronan. On his back on the bed, knees bent and spread wide to accommodate the dildo he's working in and out of his ass. He whimpers as he hits a sensitive spot.

My cock snaps to attention, going hard so fast, I swear I get a little lightheaded. Or that might just be because of the sight before me, one of my favorite fantasies brought to life. The only thing different is that I'm not the one fucking him with the dildo.

His breathing picks up, and his free hand closes around his dick, pumping it in rhythm with his thrusts. The slick gleam of lube on his skin and around the stretched pucker of his ass is the hottest fucking thing I've ever seen, and I could stand here forever, but the guilt of watching him without him knowing I'm here is too heavy a burden.

"Ronan," I rasp.

His eyes snap open, and his lust-fogged gaze lands on me. "Zac?" Then orgasm overtakes him, and he cries out as his body convulses.

Swallowing hard, I avert my gaze and go into the bathroom, giving him time to pull himself together while I dampen a towel with warm water. I deliberately take longer than I need before going back into the bedroom.

He's sitting up on the bed, the sheet held tight around his waist, dildo nowhere to be seen. I don't know where exactly to look.

"Here." I offer the towel. "I thought you might..." Belatedly, I realize there's no mess—no cum, anyway.

As if he can read my mind, he says, "Dragons don't ejaculate."

That's something to think about later. "Oh. Sorry. I didn't mean to watch. I… Zoe was at my place and insisted I come back here. And then I heard… um. Well, I th-thought you might be hurt." I'm stumbling over the words like an adolescent, and the back of my neck feels hot. "I'm sorry."

There are so many questions I want to ask him, like… have you been kicking me out every night so you can play with a dildo? *Why?* Did he think I wouldn't… or is it that he'd rather have the toy than me?

Ronan's face relaxes a little. "Zoe, huh?" He takes the towel and mutters, "I'll kill her."

I don't know what to say, so I half turn away, giving him a little privacy to clean up the lube. If I was a better person, I'd leave, but I guess I'm flawed.

The sheets rustle, and I try not to picture what Ronan's doing. What I wish I was doing for him. "You can look at me now," he says, and he sounds a lot more… confident? When I turn back, he's off the bed, wearing sweatpants and nothing else. The dildo is lying on the towel amid the rumpled sheets. It's pink—I hadn't noticed that before.

"We should talk," Ronan says. "We should have talked before now. I'm sorry."

Dread forms a lump in my throat, but I force words past it. "Are you ending things with me?"

"What? No!" His genuine shock allows me to breathe a little easier. "Zac, no. There's no way. I…" He sighs. "Wow, I really messed this up." Closing the distance between us, he takes my hands in his. "We need to talk, but I'm not ending things. Maybe this is premature, but I'm actually so far in love with you that just the thought of not having you in my life hurts every part of me."

I don't think my brain can handle this many shocks in such a short space of time. "You love me?" My hands tighten on his.

He searches my expression with a worried gaze. "Yes. I do. I love you. So, so much."

Clearing my throat, I nod. "I love you too. That's why it hurt when… This past week, you've been so happy for me to leave. I thought maybe you were getting sick of me."

The little laugh that huffs out of him is reassuring. "That's definitely not it. We need to sit down for this, I think." He glances at the bed. "Um. Would it gross you out if we stayed in here? We can go into the living room."

Ronan loves me and wants me in his bedroom? That's not something I'll say no to.

"Here is fine."

CHAPTER TWENTY-SEVEN

Ronan

This wasn't how I wanted to have this conversation, but it's all my own fault. If I'd listened to my friends and talked to Zac about this sooner, we wouldn't be doing this with me half-naked after he just watched me fuck myself with a dildo.

At least I learned that I definitely like to bottom. I was pretty sure of that after a week spent fingering myself, but I'm a hundred percent certain now. So that's information I can bring to the table. And him walking in on me means I don't have to think of a way to bring up the subject.

I'm still going to kill Zoe, though.

I climb onto the bed and sit with my legs crossed, and he perches on the edge of the mattress about a foot and a half away from me. The distance is a punch to the face, but after what he said about thinking I want to break up with him, I get it,

"I love you," I say. That's a good place to start, right? "We're still new, and we've been going slow, but I know that. Just like I know that Hortplatz is going to be my home, and when I picture my life here, it's with you." I wince. "You do get a say in that. I'm not suggesting that I plan to keep you locked in my house or anything."

He cracks a smile, and I take it as encouragement. "This last week… it wasn't about you. Well, it kind of was. I wanted to…" Shit, this is hard to say out loud. "I wanted to please you."

I've had enough practice reading demon faces that I can see the emotions playing out in his expression. He clears his throat. "Please me? So… this, tonight," he gestures to the bed and the Ding Dong Dildo, "this isn't because you're, uh, not sexually attracted to me? Because it's okay if that's it," he rushes to add. "If you're demi-sexual or asexual and sex with me isn't what you want, that's okay. We can—"

Unable to resist, I close the distance between us and kiss him. How can I not? He's perfect, and he wants me. Just me. All of me.

When I pull back, his gaze searches mine. "So… not that?"

"Not that," I confirm. "I want to have sex with you. A lot. But I'm a virgin, and I didn't want our first time to be… I don't know, *work* for you. I wanted to be able to give as good as I got. I wanted to know exactly what I liked and have some… some sexual confidence."

Understanding dawns, and then a smile tugs at his lips. "Then… this whole week, you've been sending me home so you can experiment with a dildo?"

I nod, then shake my head. "The dildo only came today. I asked my friends for advice, and they said I should talk to you." I make a face. "I should have listened to that bit. Then they sent me some helpful porn and the lube spell, told me to play with myself, and bought me some toys."

Zac's jaw drops. "That's… friendship. Uh… toys,

plural? I mean…" He shakes his head. "We can talk about that later. If you need time to p-play with yourself and toys"—his breathing is getting a little shaky—"then that's what you need. I'm happy for you to take all the time in the world, Ronan. Whatever you want. I wish you'd told me, but I guess I could have asked you what was going on instead of just freaking out."

I snort. "What you're saying is that we need to communicate better? Who would have guessed. It's not like our whole relationship hasn't been one huge miscommunication after another."

He laughs. "New rule—full disclosure. How's that sound?"

"Deal."

"Okay, so then I need to tell you… I talked to Gideon a while back. Asked him if he knew anything about your past. I didn't want to accidentally bring up bad memories for you, and I was hoping he'd have some insight."

My whole body feels like lead, and I drop my gaze to my lap. "Wh-What did he say?"

"That you had a shitty childhood and even telling me that much was enough to get us all in trouble. He said to leave it alone. And I will—I swear. But I needed to tell you because the other day I called him again to find out when your birthday is."

My head snaps up. "What?" Is *that* why Hagen was asking all those questions?

"I didn't want to ask you in case you had trauma about it, but I wanted to know if I could throw a party for you."

The grin that spreads across my face is so wide, I think it might become its own entity. "You want to throw me a birthday party?"

He nods. "A big one. It was going to be a surprise, but I can find other ways to surprise you. I think it's more important that I'm honest with you now. I went behind your back to ask questions about something I knew you didn't want to talk about."

The grin doesn't fade. For the first time ever, thinking about my past doesn't kill my mood. Why should it, when my future is so bright?

"Thank you. I promise I'll pretend to be *so* surprised at the party. I have to, because my friends think they're sneaky, and they'll be heartbroken if they find out I already know."

The last of his concern leaves his face, and he chuckles. "Not just them. Garrett's cousin Alistair is way too into this."

I've met Alistair a few times. The first, he was scary. But he's a friend of Wil's, and once Wil accepted me, it flipped a switch for Alistair. We're not friends, but he's been friendly to me. Though apparently he's that way with most people he meets.

Taking Zac's hand, I say quietly, "I really can't tell you much about my past. Gideon's right—you already know more than you should. And I didn't have it too bad while I was living it—the worst came when I realized what I'd been denied. When I realized that I'd done things I'll never stop regretting. I never had a birthday—I don't even know when I was hatched, exactly. So I've chosen one. And I want to share it with my family and friends every damn year, because I don't have to spend the rest of my life in the prison *he* made me." I've said too much, but from the way Zac's face sets, I know he'd never give me away. Never betray my secret.

"Gideon said he's dead."

I nod. "Yes."

"Then every year, we celebrate your birthday and spit on his memory. Every *day*."

A tear runs down my cheek. "Every day." I swipe away the liquid, then smile at him. "Including today. How do you feel about deflowering a virgin?"

A laugh bursts from him. "*Deflowering?*"

"Fabian bookmarked some of the porn videos with comments, and that was one of them." I shrug. "Does it not mean what I think?"

"It does, but it's old-fashioned. And usually used for women."

I smirk at him. "So you don't want my flower?"

His mouth crashes down on mine in a devouring kiss that has me hard as a spike again in seconds. "Oh, I want it," he growls. "But only when you're ready."

"I'm ready." So, so ready. "I'm even still prepped. Full disclosure: I love having something hard in my ass."

Zac swallows. "You're sure?" he whispers.

I lift a hand to cup his cheek. "Let's start our life together."

His smile is the most beautiful thing I've ever seen, and he kisses me again, this time more gently. I fist my hands in his shirt and let myself topple back against the pillows, drawing him down with me to lie between my legs, then frown and plant my hands on his chest. "Nope. Up." I push gently, and he immediately retreats.

"What's wrong?"

"You're not naked." I give him the big-eyed pout Cam uses on Micah. I'm not sure if it works or if he just recognizes that getting naked is to both our benefit, but he scrambles off the bed and attacks his belt buckle. "Slower," I demand. "I want to see you strip for me."

Zac pauses and meets my gaze. Whatever he sees there makes him grin. "Looking for some entertainment, are you?"

I wrap my hand around my dick and stroke, drawing

his eyes to it. They widen. "Huh. Dragon dick is different from what I thought."

"Impress me, and you can play."

He sucks in a sharp breath and slowly peels up the bottom of his shirt. I've seen his bare chest before, but somehow, this time it's different. The shadows cast by the bedside lamp play over the slabs of hard muscle as they're revealed, inch by inch, until he pulls it over his head and tosses it to the side.

"Impressed yet?"

I squeeze my cock and try not to let my voice shake. "N-Nothing I haven't seen before."

"I guess I'll just have to do better." His hands go to his waist and unbuckle his belt. He pulls it free, and I have a sudden flash of one porn clip I saw... but I'm not ready for that.

Yet.

My attention is glued to his every movement as he unfastens the button and slooooowly drags down the zip. He kicks off his shoes, and a second later, his pants fall to the floor. Never before have I seen someone look graceful while stepping out of pants. Not that I've ever seen anyone else step out of their pants, but I know *I'm* not graceful when I do it.

I can't believe I'm thinking about his grace when the bulge in his briefs is right there. My throat goes dry. "Take them off," I whisper.

He slides his thumbs into the waistband. "These?"

I nod.

"Hmm. I'm not sure. Are you suitably impressed?" He skims a broad palm over his hard, fabric-covered cock and shudders. I do the same, imagining that same hand on me.

"So far..."

He grins and loses the briefs. "What about now? Any better?"

I can't muster the words to reply, only a hungry, animalistic sound that bursts from me at the sight of his huge dick. Coke can? I get it now. The tip is glistening with precum, and I can't wait to taste it. Taste him. I'm on my knees in front of him before I can think that through.

"Ronan?" His voice hitches.

"Tell me if I do something wrong." I wrap my lips around the head, stretching them wide. There's no way I'm getting much more of him into my mouth—not without a lot of practice—but from the sound he makes, I don't think he cares.

"Love," he breathes, his hands coming to my hair, and the endearment makes me melt. Determinedly, I work a little more of him inside, using my tongue to massage the underside and loving the way his groan vibrates through his whole body. This is so different from how I'd imagined —I didn't take into account the way it would exercise muscles in my jaw that aren't used to it, or that he'd be so solid and warm… yet his skin is softer there than anywhere else.

Tentatively, not wanting to hurt him, I suck, and his hands tighten in my hair. "Yeah, love. Like that."

Encouraged, I do it again, withdrawing slightly to adjust, trying not to catch him with my teeth. It's hard, but I guess he's used to it, because he doesn't flinch, only eggs me on.

When his thigh muscles are trembling and the low, muttered exclamations of pleasure stop, I lift my gaze, searching for validation. His eyes are squeezed shut, but then he opens them and looks at me, and there's so much love and lust there that I would happily drown in it.

"Let's move to the bed," he says hoarsely. "I'm not

going to last, and I want you to come too. We can sixty-nine or—"

I pull off him and wipe the back of my hand over my mouth. "I want you to fuck me."

He stops talking, and his throat works. "Are you sure?"

"Very." I get up, feeling new confidence, and grab his hand. "Fuck me now, so I can see your face when you come. Then, when we've taken the edge off, we can do everything else." I lean in to kiss him. "And, Zac, I want to do *everything.*"

He hauls me against him, kissing me so hard, I'll feel it for days, and I *love* it. "How did I get this lucky?" he mutters against my mouth. I want to make him feel that way for the rest of our lives.

We turn to the bed, and he orders, "Your turn to get naked."

Obediently, I drop my sweatpants, then crawl up onto the mattress, hesitating. Maybe I should stay on my hands and knees? But no—I really do want to see his face this first time. We can change positions later.

Lying back against the pillows, I draw him down to me. His face goes to the crook of my neck, planting kisses there, down over my collarbone.

"Stop," I insist. "Fuck first. Play later."

He laughs. "That's not romantic, Ronan. I thought you wanted our first time to be special?"

I shrug. "I'm with you. It's already the most special thing in the world."

His gaze heats. "I love you."

Those three words that nobody has ever said to me before I came to Hortplatz mean more than anything I ever had before. "I love you. Now fuck me."

"Where's your lube?" He looks over at the nightstand.

"Hold out your hand." When he does, I pull on a

thread of my magic and spell a small puddle of lube into his palm. He blinks at it, then lifts his gaze to me.

"This is going to come in handy."

"Pun intended?"

"What—oh." He grins. "Sure. That was definitely on purpose. Open your legs."

I bend my knees and let them fall open, and my cock points at him in eager anticipation. He bends to lay a kiss on it, then checks to make sure I'm properly prepared—which I am, thanks to my friend Ding Dong—and slicks the remaining lube over himself, positioning his Coke can cock. It nudges against me, and I tremble with restrained desperation.

"Ready?" Zac asks quietly, and I nod.

I thought the dildo stretched me, but I was so, so wrong. This… this is what stretching feels like. It's a little uncomfortable, even though he's going slow, but when he pauses, I wrap my arms around his shoulders. "Do *not* stop."

"I'm not. Just giving you time to get used to me." His words are rough, and there's sweat forming at his hairline. I did this to him.

Experimentally, I adjust my hips, sending him an inch deeper and making us both gasp. "Ronan," he warns.

"I'm okay," I assure him. "Just need you." And it's true. My body's adjusting, relaxing, welcoming him, and as it does, my desire comes raging back.

"Slowly," he repeats, and I let him set the pace.

I feel the subtle change in him when he's all the way in, the way his muscles seem to relax, then tense for an entirely different reason. "Okay?" he asks, searching my face.

"Perfect," I assure him. "Can I move?"

"If you want to." I do, flexing my hips again, and he groans. "I take it back. Just… lie there. Or I'll die."

I suppress a laugh, lifting my head slightly to bite his earlobe. "Make me come, Zac. I want to come with you in me."

He shifts his weight to one arm and reaches between us to grab my dick. "Ridged," he mumbles. "I like it." Then he begins the torment, his cock withdrawing slightly only to plunge back in—in perfect rhythm with his hand stroking me. The barrage of sensation is more than I'd expected, and I gasp.

At first, he keeps a steady pace, working every nerve with slow deliberation, but when my breathing becomes unsteady and my head starts to thrash, he picks up speed.

"Zac," I moan.

"I've got you, love. Come for me."

A sob escapes me. I want to, want to, want to—

It takes me without warning, seizing every muscle until I'm sure I'll die. Distantly, I hear Zac's shout and pry open eyes I didn't realize were closed so I can see his face. It's clenched in the same agonizing rictus of pleasure I feel, and I let go, roll with it, happy in the knowledge that Zac is my future.

CHAPTER TWENTY-EIGHT

Zac

THERE IS nothing quite so amazing as waking up with Ronan's body tangled in mine. Memories of last night play in my head as I swim toward consciousness, tightening my arms around him, and I can feel myself smiling. He was worried about pleasing me? How could I ever be unhappy with a partner who wants me as much as he does?

How could I ever be unhappy with Ronan?

"Good morning," he murmurs, and I open my eyes. He's smiling at me from our shared pillow, a smile full of naughty secrets and love. There's no doubt in my mind that I want to wake up this way every day for the rest of my life.

"Hi. How are you feeling today?" After that first time —which was actually the second time he'd had something in his ass last night—we brought out the toys. I offered to be Ronan's live test body, but he insisted on using the Fleshlight first to make sure he could make it good for me. I didn't bother to point out that the Fleshlight wouldn't know if it was good or not—Ronan being stubborn is adorable, and it was no hardship to jerk myself and watch him fuck the toy. After which he decided he was definitely versatile and fucked me. Then we took a shower together and he ordered me to teach him the finer points of how to give a blowjob.

He's an excellent student.

Moving against me, he winces a little. "I'm discovering muscles I didn't know I had. And some of the other ones are sore too."

I'm instantly contrite. "We probably did too much for your first time. I'm sorry. A hot shower might help, and a massage?"

He scoots closer to kiss me. "No, I like it. It's a tangible reminder of everything we did. I could heal it if I wanted to, but for now, I'm keeping all the soreness as a trophy of my deflowering."

I laugh, the same way I do every time he says that word —and he's said it a few times now. He seems to enjoy my reaction. "I think your flower is supposed to be the trophy, and that's mine," I tease.

"I've been thinking about that…" His tone is thoughtful, but overly so. As though he's putting it on. "Since the Ding Dong Dildo was there first, does it have my flower?"

With mock outrage, I roll him under me. "Are you saying it 'rang your bell' better than I did?"

Laughing, his eyes dancing with happiness, he shrugs. "All I'm saying is that Ding Dong was the first."

I steal a kiss and adopt the same fake, thoughtful tone as him. "Maybe we should ask your friends what they think."

"Oh fuck no. I'll never hear the end of it. My flower is yours. Ding Dong will just have to deal with second place."

We stay like that, kissing under the warm comforter in the peace of an early Sunday morning, until things start to get more heated. That's when I roll away.

"What? Nooooo. Zac," he whines.

"Not unless you heal yourself first."

His eyes narrow stubbornly. "But I like the ache."

"Then you can wait until tonight for sex." Even if he doesn't heal himself, I know the natural metabolic rate of a dragon will mean he'll be a lot less sore by then. Not like a human, who might need a few days.

"Fine. Just remember that if I'm waiting, so are you. So I guess that means I can't practice my blowjobs this morning." He gets out of bed and strolls toward the bathroom—or at least, I think that's what he's aiming for. Instead, it's initially a stagger, then a half-limping gait. I still enjoy the sight of his naked back as it goes.

ᔕᘻ

AROUND MIDMORNING, we're in the kitchen, me cleaning up after our breakfast of fresh cinnamon rolls (and when I say fresh, I mean I watched Ronan make the dough and had to wait for it to rise—twice) and fruit while Ronan sits at the table, paging through one of the ancient recipe books someone let him borrow and making notes. There's a little furrow between his brows as he asks, "How difficult would it be to get a wood-burning oven up here? Would I need a permit?"

I shrug. "Depends on where you want to put it. I don't think the courtyard you have here is big enough to meet the fire regulations." The townhouse we arranged for him was designed to be low maintenance.

He pouts. "Damn."

Drying the last bowl, I slot it neatly into the cupboard. "But the yard at my place is. Or we could ask around town, see if someone who has one would let you use it."

His nod is clearly disappointed. "That's probably the sensible option."

The doorbell rings, and I toss the dishtowel onto the counter. "I'll get it." It's probably Zoe, come to beg forgiveness from both of us for her little trick last night. I wonder if she's sorry enough to let me install a wood-burning oven for Ronan in her yard.

I'm planning the best way to frame the argument when I open the door and see my grandmother.

"You're not Zoe," I say, my intelligence fleeing.

"No, I am not."

We stare at each other. What's she doing here? Normally if she wants to see me, she calls and I go to her. I can't even remember the last time she visited our house— and I know for sure she's never come to the front door and rung the bell. Though, I suppose this is Ronan's house, not mine, so maybe...

"Are we going to stand here all day?" she asks acerbically, and I shake off my brain fog.

"No. Come in." I step back so she can pass me, then gesture toward the living room. If she's here to cause trouble, I can kick her out. I can. But in the meantime, I'm not leaving my nine-centuries-old grandmother standing in the cold on the doorstep. "Would you like a drink? Or a cinnamon roll?"

She sniffs, and at first I think she's being derogatory, but then she says, "Is that what I can smell?"

"Uh... yes. Ronan baked this morning."

"I ate not long ago, but I could be convinced to take one home with me."

My jaw drops, and I snap my mouth closed. Has she taken a blow to the head? "Of course," I manage. "I'll—"

"Zac?" Ronan calls, coming down the hall. "Who is it?"

Part of me wishes he'd stayed safely in the kitchen, but I'm also so grateful he's here to rescue me. He steps into the living room, and his smile vanishes as his gaze lands on Grandmother.

"Damaris," he says. "This is a surprise." He glances at me questioningly, and I shrug.

"Yes. I knew Zac would be here, and I need to speak with him." She sits in one of the armchairs, and Ronan's lips twitch. Anyone else might be irritated by her audacity, but of course my dragon finds it funny.

"I'll leave you to it, then," he says, then squeezes my arm. "I'm just in the kitchen." It's as much a warning for Grandmother as it is reassurance for me.

"You should stay," she says, surprising us both.

"I should?"

One of her brows rises in that expression I know so well. "You and Zac are together now, correct? Or have I been misinformed?"

Annoyed, I take Ronan's hand and lead him to the couch. "You haven't been misinformed." To him, I add, "Full disclosure, remember? I would've told you later anyway, so you may as well stay."

He just smiles and squeezes my hand, and we both turn to look at Grandmother. She's watching us closely, but her face is unreadable.

"I came to apologize."

The shock that reverberates through me this time is too much to recover from. Apologize? *Grandmother?* No. This isn't a thing that happens.

She's still talking, though. Saying things that don't make sense.

"I should have taken the time to listen to your idea. You're my grandson, I love you, and I value you. You deserved that from me."

An awkward little silence falls. I don't know what to say… It's possible I've lost the power to speak, even. Luckily, Ronan is with me.

"Why didn't you listen?" he asks quietly. "And why continue to deny the validity of the resort? Surely you don't still think it's a bad idea?"

"I never thought it was a bad idea," she admits, and I make a choking sound.

"Then *why*?" I spit. "*Why* did you shut me down? Why insist on not supporting us? Why did Ronan have to blackmail you?" That last comes out on a half sob, and Ronan's grip on my hand tightens.

For a long time, she says nothing. Then she glances away and sighs before meeting my gaze squarely. "I panicked."

What?

"You were so excited and passionate about this idea that would bring more visitors here, and I panicked."

Ronan nods. "You're unsure about opening Hortplatz to outsiders."

Grandmother shakes her head. "No, that must happen. It was remiss of me not to see that decades ago."

I exchange a glance with Ronan. Okay, so if not that…?

"You were afraid the influx of people would show Zac what he was missing and he'd want to leave?" Ronan guesses, but Grandmother shakes her head again.

"The opposite."

Maybe she really has suffered a blow to the head.

"I don't understand," I croak. "Grandmother…"

"Asher and Micah are so happy now. I saw them both newly in love and settled and happy with their lives, and I was thrilled. Nobody believes it of me, but what I've always wanted most is for my family to be safe and happy."

"I believe it," I manage.

"So do I," Ronan adds. "That's why we were all so shocked about the ski resort."

Grandmother nods. "Your cousins falling in love was a *fluke*. That the perfect partners for them should happen to come to Hortplatz… the odds are ridiculous. I wanted that same happiness for you, but I knew you'd be resistant to me matchmaking, and the chances of you meeting someone here were so small, Zac. I was trying to think of a way to get you out of the village for a while. I thought perhaps the museum would help—that you'd meet academics who'd traveled the world and hear their stories and want to see those places."

I could argue that I have seen a lot of places—I've lived in various countries while studying multiple times over the centuries. Done fieldwork in a lot of different places; met a lot of people. But I don't want to interrupt. I've never heard her speak so openly before.

"And then you came and told me you had this idea for a ski resort, and I panicked. A project like that would keep you here, make you happy, and I wanted… I didn't want you to be unhappy, but I wanted you to need to stretch your wings. I knew you'd never go as long as you thought you were needed here. Of all my grandchildren, you're the most like me."

"What? No, that's Gideon," I exclaim, startled.

She snorts. "Gideon has my temperament. Our little murder baby," she murmurs, sounding almost fond. "But Gideon left, Zac. Gideon will always care about our family and community, and he'll always do his part, but he also knows his boundaries and enforces them. You, on the other hand… you're like me. You'll keep giving and worrying for as long as you're needed. And we'll always be needed."

I'm pretty sure she just called me a pushover, but she also included herself in that category, so I can't be mad.

"So you tried to shut down the project because you wanted Zac to do something for himself instead of for the village," Ronan concludes.

"Yes. The ski resort is an excellent idea. It will make an enormous difference here, and I'm so proud of you—all of you. But I wanted you to have a similar experience to me in my youth. I spent over a hundred years away from our community, living with others and learning new things and falling in love. Your grandfather was the best thing that ever happened in my life. He challenged me, loved me, and stood by my side in every fight. The thought that you might not be able to have the opportunity to find that terrified me." She takes a deep breath. "And then your dragon blackmailed me."

"His name is Ronan." After everything he's been through to establish his identity, I'm not letting anyone take that from him.

"I know. Ronan blackmailed me because he wanted you to have your dream. It… gave me hope. I thought if you two were together, maybe you'd leave with him."

Ronan shakes his head. "I'm not leaving."

"So I've heard. But Zac's setting boundaries now. His presentation to the village council about needing a team to support him as the village grows was a positive sign for me. He let Asher shout at me." She looks at me, and a tiny smile curls her lips. "You snapped at me. These weeks you've been with Ronan and planning for your resort have changed you."

"There were easier ways to get me to find a life, Grandmother. Not volunteering me for every job that came up would have been one of them."

"Perhaps. I kept waiting for you to say no and leave,

but you never did. I know I played a part in all this—I knew I could depend on you, and so I asked too much when I should have known better. I apologize for that, Zac."

"Thank you." Her apology means more to me than I expected it to. She was still wrong to handle things the way she did, but having her acknowledge that makes a difference. "In future, if you have concerns about my life or anyone else's, you should discuss that with us instead of making unilateral decisions."

Her eyes narrow. I may have pushed things too far, but I hold her gaze, and she grudgingly nods. Then she turns her attention to Ronan. "If you truly mean to settle here, I believe you may be interested in the knowledge that several of our councilors are planning to retire next year. I've already spoken to Garrett."

I'm still reeling from the implication that she wants Ronan on the village council when she stands and says, "I'll take that cinnamon roll now and see you both at dinner tonight."

EPILOGUE

Ronan

THREE YEARS LATER

Fireworks explode overhead in the shape of a green dragon, and I grin. Zac's really gone all out this year. The dragon even kind of looks like me.

He slings an arm over my shoulders. "Happy Birthday, my dragon."

Taking my eyes off the sky for a second, I kiss him. "Thank you. For everything." It would take me a month to list off exactly what's included in that "everything," but it starts with the incredible birthday party he's thrown me and finishes with the way he loves me.

"You're worth everything." He leans his head against mine, and for a few minutes, we stand in our own little bubble, watching the stunning light show.

Then Zac straightens. "What— No, Alistair! What did I say about the glitter cannon? It's for *after* the fireworks." His arm drops from my shoulders, and he disappears into the crowd to deal with our annoying but loveable cousin-by-proxy. That title was Alistair's idea, and we eventually gave in just to stop the constant messages about it.

The space beside me is filled a moment later by someone my magic immediately recognizes, and I shoot my brother a smile. He's looking a little less on edge than I expected, given the size of the crowd.

"Thanks for coming," I tell him.

He makes a noncommittal sound. "It's your birthday, and it's important to you." Glancing around, he begrudgingly adds, "I like it here."

I laugh. "Me too."

"Are you coming to visit this summer?"

"Hmm." I shrug. "For a couple of weeks, sure. I don't know when yet, though. Even though it's the off-season, it's already looking busier than we expected." The ski resort opened exactly as we planned, and just like Zoe said, was an instant hit. The first winter, before everything was completely up and running, we were mostly hosting the academics who'd come to see the vault and its contents. Garrett and I were run off our feet giving tours and supervising private visits, but the word of what we'd found spread really fast, even before the combined governments began promoting it. Before the winter ended, Garrett was recruiting people to work in the museum. We eventually decided to build a custom facility just outside the village to properly house all the historic treasures, and had replicas made to showcase in the vault. That allows us to split crowds in half and show them one place at a time.

Between the academic groups who desperately want to study everything and the families who like to ooh and aah over how *old* everything is and how *amazing* the vault door is before they hit the ski slopes, the past two winters have changed everything.

Garrett managed to hire a whole team of elves with

the ability to operate portals. We were so hung up on our concern that those people primarily worked for the government that we overlooked a key factor—now that the elves are settled on Earth, where there isn't the constant threat of destruction, the government has less need for portals. The DEA, with the approval of Brandt and the elf king, was very happy to introduce a new transition-to-retirement program, whereby portal-capable elves could volunteer to be seconded to work in Hortplatz for a year. If they decide they like it, they can officially retire from the DEA and be hired by the village council or the museum on a permanent basis. If they hate it, they transfer out of the program after a year. The best part for us is, that first year is paid for by the DEA as part of their financial obligation to the museum. Both governments decided to leave all the items found in the vault in the museum, which is funded jointly by them and Hortplatz.

So now the village has regular, instant transportation to and from Zurich. Technically the elves can open the portals anywhere, but we decided early on that we didn't want a confusing free-for-all. Just like trains, buses, and planes, transport into Hortplatz runs on a schedule and a ticket is required—and proof of accommodation. The last thing we need is idiot tourists deciding to take a chance that they can find something when they get here and then freezing in the street because they can't.

When I say "we," I'm referring to the Hortplatz village council, of which I'm a member. If I want what's best for this community, I need to be a decision-making voice. Garrett declined Damaris's not-so-subtle prodding at first, but then last year another seat opened up, and I railroaded him into it. None of the Bailey cousins are that interested in local government—they prefer to look after the village in other ways. So I figure Garrett and I can be the next generation of politicians in the family. Damaris approves.

"I'm glad you've found your place," Steffen says. "You're happy."

"You are too. It's good that we get that."

He holds my gaze, his face so like mine, and a hint of a smile curls his mouth. "We win."

We do. Éibhear can't hurt us anymore. I can even use his name now without mentally flinching.

"It warms me inside to see you both like this," a familiar voice declares, and in unison Steffen and I turn as Brandt approaches us. He's weaving a little.

"Did you take a drink from Alistair?" Steffen demands.

Brandt hiccups. "Not just one! That hellhound has a real gift for parties. The booze has glitter in it!"

"I told you not to drink that," my brother gripes. "Who knows what his brewer puts in it?"

"Plus, it's alcoholic enough to take you down in dragon form," I add. I know because the last time Alistair came to visit, he brought some with him, and he, Garrett, Zoe, Cam, and I had a middle-of-the-night trial run to see if it would actually affect me in dragon form. After five drinks, I couldn't even see straight enough to launch, much less fly. I changed back into biped form and lay in the snow, giggling with my friends until Zac came to carry me home.

The suspicious glance Steffen slides me suggests he thinks I might know more than I'm saying, and I try to look innocent. My brother definitely wouldn't approve of that night.

"Tipsish is fun, though," Brandt says, then sighs. "But I have to talk to you, so…" His magic electrifies the air around us, and in the next moment, he's completely sober. "Well, that's sad. I'm definitely going to speak to Alistair about getting some of that champagne for home."

Steffen glares, then stomps off, muttering about annoying hellhounds.

"He's mellowed so much," Brandt says fondly, watching him go. Then he turns to me. "And you! Look how you've come into your own. I'm so proud of you, Ronan."

My whole body warms with the praise. There's nothing quite like the connection we dragons feel with our wing leader, and having him be proud of me is second only to having Zac love me.

"I know you weren't happy about coming here, in the beginning," he continues, keeping his voice low enough that the throngs of people around us can't overhear. "You thought I was punishing you."

I grimace. "Not punishing, exactly. You wouldn't do that. But I didn't feel suited to the task. I didn't feel like I was a real dragon, not like everyone else. And I considered it part of my atonement for… everything."

"Do you still?"

The idea is so ridiculous that I laugh. "I did things that I'll always regret, but when I did them, it was genuinely because I thought I was doing right. I never deliberately hurt anyone for the sake of it. And what Éibhear did… that's not my burden to carry. I don't have anything left to atone for, just a good life to live."

Brandt smiles widely. "This is what I like to hear. You *are* a 'real' dragon, Ronan. You always have been. I sent you here because I knew you'd be equal to the task, that you'd treat the precious treasure with the respect it deserved, and that, away from other dragons, you'd be able to find yourself without making so many comparisons. It broke my heart to see how lost you were. Being raised in a dragon family isn't what it takes to be a dragon—you just *are*."

"I know that now." I sigh. "I wish I had a hoard, though. That's something I still haven't found."

His mouth turns down in a frown. "Are you sure? The life force seems to think that's wrong."

I blink, startled. "I'd know, wouldn't I? I don't have a room full of things I've colle…"

A silvering eyebrow rises. "Thought of something?"

Feeling a little foolish, I nod. "Recipes. I didn't even realize, but these last few years… since I decided to let myself be who I wanted to…"

"You started baking," Brandt prompts. "I remember. My stomach appreciates your care packages."

"And I've been gathering recipes to try. I have a whole bookcase full of them, and cloud storage too. The other week Zac said he'd get me another bookcase for the ones that are piling up on the kitchen table." I face-palm. "How did I not notice?"

He pats my shoulder reassuringly. "This is usually how it starts, and you don't have a bunch of nosy dragons here to point it out. What's your reaction if I suggest you throw out some of those recipes?"

The hiss takes me by surprise, but Brandt laughs. "Yep. Definitely your hoard. Congratulations. Before you know it, you'll need a special room for it."

I smile smugly and make a mental note to tell Zac. He'll get Micah started on drawing up plans for an extension to the house.

"Ronan, you'll always be welcome at Here Be Dragons," Brandt says, suddenly solemn. "But I'm thrilled to see the home you've made here."

"Cake time!" someone shouts, and the guests burst into cheers. The crowd parts to make way for me, and ahead, I see Zac smiling from behind the long trestle with the cake on it. A cake I made. Zac protested that nobody should have to make their own birthday cake, but as I said, when else would I have the chance to make an eighteen-inch-high, four-foot-long cake in the shape of a dragon? He insisted that he would help, at least, and that gave me even more amazing memories. There's no room for bad ones anymore, just happy ones with my friends and Zac. Here, in my home… where I finally belong.

Time to blow out my birthday candles.

Я

Thanks for reading *Zachary*! This brings the Demons-In-Law series to an end, and I'm so sad to say goodbye. To read the deleted scene where Ronan takes Zac flying for the first time, subscribe here: bit.ly/LouisaMBonus
If you got this far and haven't read Ronan's origin story (or the books about Gideon, Alistair, Fabian, Dustin, Brandt, and Steffen), then there's a whole world waiting for you! It all starts with *Demons Do It Better*.
We talk spoilers and updates in my Facebook reader group, RoMMance with Becca & Louisa.
And if you just can't wait for release day, check out my Patreon (patreon.com/user?u=84207502) for early access to chapters, artwork, and other bonus material, including exclusive serials!

ALSO BY LOUISA MASTERS

The Collective

Higher Demon

Demons-In-Law

Asher

Micah

Zachary

Franklin U

Mr. Romance

The Holigay Hookup *related novella

Ghostly Guardians

Spirited Situation

Vortex Conundrum

Conduit Crisis

Gateway Catastrophe

Here Be Dragons

Dragon Ever After

The Professor's Dragon

The Dragon Experiment

Conspiracy of Dragons

Hidden Species

Demons Do It Better

One Bite With A Vampire

Hijinks With A Hellhound

Sorcerers Always Satisfy

Hidden Species Box Set

Met His Match

<u>Charming Him</u>

<u>Offside Rules</u>

<u>A Christmas Chance (novella)</u>

<u>Between the Covers (M/F)</u>

Joy Universe

I've Got This

<u>Follow My Lead</u>

<u>In Your Hands</u>

<u>Take Us There</u>

Novellas

Fake It 'Til You Make It (permafree)

One Golden Night

O Hell, All Ye Shoppers

Out of the Office

After the Blaze

Blokes Down Under Novella Collection

ABOUT THE AUTHOR

Louisa Masters started reading romance much earlier than her mother thought she should. While other teenagers were sneaking out of the house, Louisa was sneaking romance novels in and working out how to read them without being discovered. As an adult, she feeds her addiction in every spare second. She spent years trying to build a "sensible" career, working in bookstores, recruitment, resource management, administration, and as a travel agent, before finally conceding defeat and devoting herself to the world of romance novels.

Louisa has a long list of places first discovered in books that she wants to visit, and every so often she overcomes her loathing of jet lag and takes a trip that charges her imagination. She lives in Melbourne, Australia, where she whines about the weather for most of the year while secretly admitting she'll probably never move.

http://www.louisamasters.com